THE NAUGHTY list

SHERIDAN ANNE

Sheridan Anne
THE NAUGHTY LIST

Copyright © 2023 Sheridan Anne
All rights reserved
First Published in 2023

This book is a work of fiction. Names, characters, places, and incidents are products of the author's imagination. Any resemblance to actual events or persons, living or dead, is entirely coincidental.

No part of this book may be reproduced, stored in a retrieval system, or transmitted in any form or by any means, without prior permission in writing of the publisher, nor be otherwise circulated in any form of the binding or cover other than in which it is published, and without a similar condition, including this condition, being imposed on the subsequent purchaser.

Cover Design: Sheridan Anne
Editing: Fox Proof Editing

Formatting: Sheridan Anne

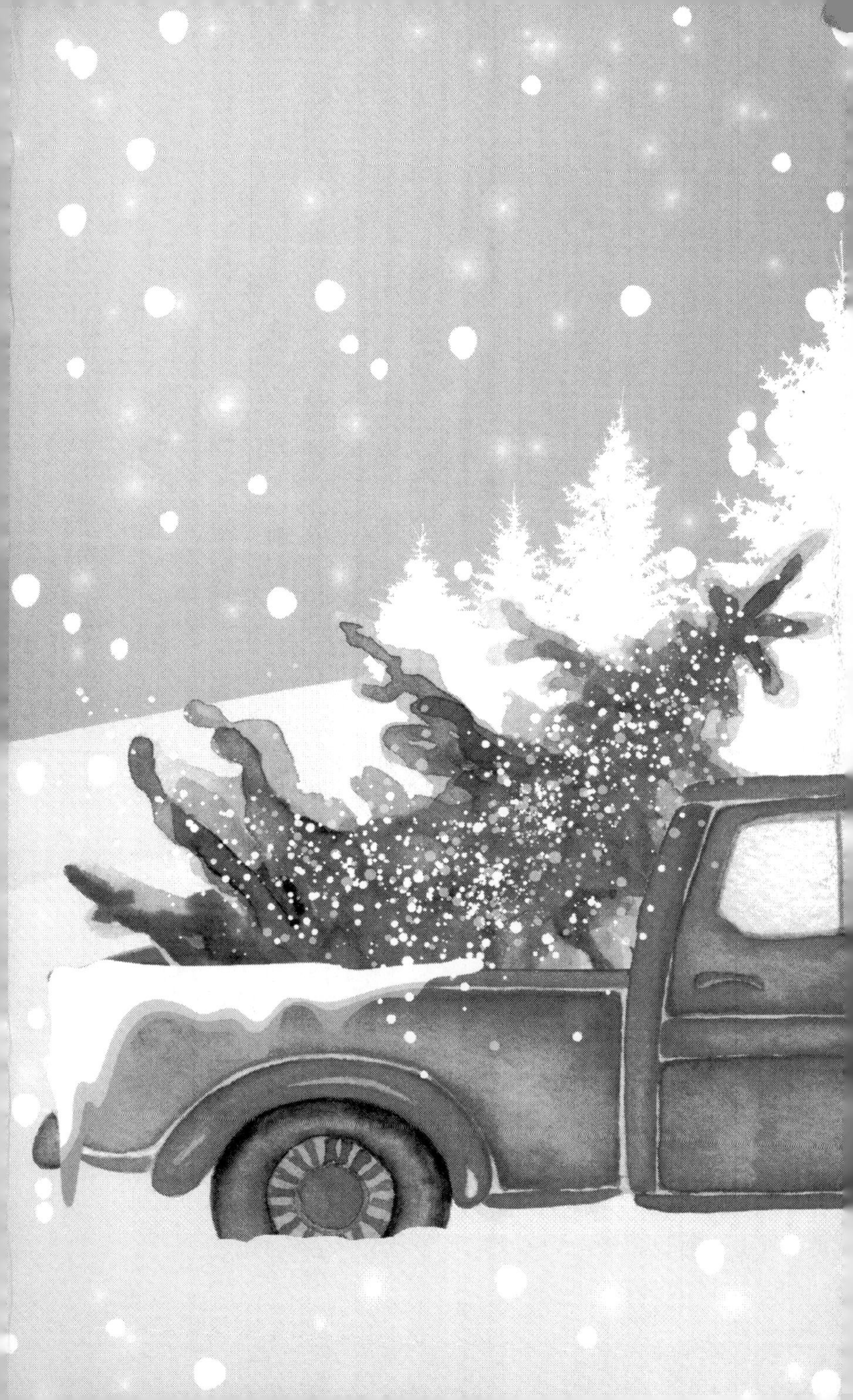

CHAPTER ONE
BLAIR

"FIRED?" I screech, my jaw hanging open in shock as I gape at my boss. "What the hell, Dwayne? I thought I was coming in here to accept a promotion. You know, the one you've been promising me for the past two years. The one I more than deserve."

"A promotion?" Dwayne grunts, gaping right back. "Be serious, Blair. How could you possibly think you were going to get that promotion? You sent a meme of a donkey getting fucked to the whole company with the caption, 'When life gets you down, find an ass to fuck.' And as if that wasn't enough, you had to include our entire client list as well. Do you have any idea how many people are on that mailing list?"

I resist the urge to roll my eyes, almost certain that at this point, there's really not much I could say to save what's left of my career. "That meme was hilarious," I deadpan, watching as the corner of his mustache-covered lip twitches with irritation. But what's new? Dwayne and I have had a love-hate relationship since the day I started at SC Corporate Management almost six years ago. "Everybody loved it. Besides, management has everyone walking on eggshells. Our clients and our team needed a good laugh and a reminder that not all of us here have our heads shoved so far up our asses that all we can smell is the foul stench of our own shit."

He gives me a blank stare. "It was inappropriate."

"Inappropriate is trying to match a striped peach tie with a salmon button-down, but you don't see me trying to have you fired over it," I mutter, arching a brow and trying to resist the urge to drop to my knees and sob. But hell, if I'm going to go down, I might as well go down swinging.

"Start packing your things, Blair," Dwayne says, striding around his oversized desk and putting an end to our conversation. "You have fifteen minutes to get yourself sorted out, and if you can't do that, I'll have no choice but to have security escort you out."

"Security?" I blanch. "Is that really necessary?"

Dwayne makes a show of gazing down at his watch. "Make that fourteen minutes."

Fuck me. If I didn't like these heels so much, I would have shoved one up his scrawny ass by now. Assuming there's enough space with his head already up there.

Knowing damn well that Dwayne will follow through on his threat, just for the purpose of getting to humiliate me in front of my colleagues one final time, I clench my jaw and turn on my heel, stalking out of his office.

This isn't exactly the first time I've been fired, and not even the first time I've been fired for sending inappropriate memes, but it's certainly the first time he's been such an ass about it. Truth be told, I'm one of the best publicists here, and the second our clientele finds out I've been kicked to the curb, there's going to be heat on Dwayne's ass to do the right thing and bring me back.

Dwayne might be my boss, but the clients we work for look to me for guidance. They barely tolerate Dwayne, and it's easy to see why. Hell, he probably only fired me so that he doesn't have to give me my Christmas bonus, and being only two weeks before Christmas, I could have really used the cash.

This time though, I'm not sure I'll be coming back, even after Dwayne pulls his head out of his ass and comes begging. Working for SC Corporate Management has always been a dream of mine, and the day I got the call that my application had been successful, I gave up my whole world to fly halfway across the country and start this new life here in New York. I got myself a cute apartment and made it my own, figured out where all the best coffee shops are, met some amazing friends, and of course, adopted one of the best nail technicians in the city.

Work was insane, but it was exactly what I was searching for. I flourished in my position and quickly worked my way up the food chain to become one of the crucial members of this incredible company. Only now, the thrill I used to get every morning I walked through the doors doesn't quite seem so bright anymore.

Maybe it's time for a change and Dwayne's bullshit is actually a blessing in disguise. Hell, maybe it's time to start my own PR firm. I've always thought about it but never had the balls to take such a big step. I'm only twenty-eight, and though there's still plenty for me to learn about this insane business, I have the connections. There are plenty of clients who will happily follow and support me.

Shit. This is New York. What hope do I have when it comes to starting my own firm and competing against these huge powerhouse businesses? I'm kidding myself thinking I could do this.

Stopping by the storeroom, I grab a cardboard box and make my way back to my office. I mutter a string of ridiculous insults as I go, and with every step I take, I can't help but feel the eyes of my colleagues on my back. They all saw the meme. Hell, most of them were laughing with me about it first thing this morning, but the second I was called into Dwayne's office, they all knew what was going to happen. I suppose I did too, but I didn't want to believe the asshole was that petty.

Who am I kidding? Of course he is.

I've always had an open-door policy, but as I walk into my office, I pull the door closed behind me, needing privacy from the prying eyes as I drop the cardboard box onto my disorganized desk. I've got way too much work to do to have to worry about being fired, but I suppose it's somebody else's work to handle now. It's no longer my problem.

A heavy weight settles into my chest. I like this stuff being my problem.

Damn it.

Dropping my ass to my desk chair, I search through my drawers and grab all of my personal stuff before dropping them into the box, then just to be an ass, I take the potted plant and put it in too. Once the drawers have been emptied, I work on my desk, and my gaze settles on the picture of me and my nana from my college graduation nearly six years ago. She was always my biggest supporter, even if it meant having to deal with the insane distance. Two weeks after this photo was taken, I was gone.

All Nana wanted was for me to be happy in what I was doing, though there's no denying it, she was worried about my heart. When I left for New York, giving up my home wasn't all I walked away from.

Nicholas Stone.

He was my high school boyfriend and was everything to me. Nick was my first real love, and having to walk away from that left one hell of a scar on my heart. I think a part of me will always love him, but that's ancient history now. We were together right until the day I left, but during those college years, it was tough.

The distance never really worked for us, and I could feel the castle we'd built around us beginning to crumble. Calling it quits was the most difficult decision I've ever made, but had we continued, we would have ended up hating each other, and I couldn't bear the thought of that happening to the man I was so deeply in love with. It was time to go, and tearing myself away from him destroyed me in a way I've never truly recovered from.

It's been nearly six years since I last laid eyes on him, and honestly, he's a big part of the reason why I haven't headed back to our beautiful small town of Blushing, Colorado since the day I left. But Nana has nothing to worry about—at least, she didn't. She passed away in her sleep last month, and due to the ridiculous amount of work I have going on here, I couldn't make it back to Blushing for her funeral. I regret my decision not to go, and truth be told, I think the day Dwayne denied my application to take personal leave was where this downward spiral at work began. I had respect for Dwayne before he denied my leave, and since then, all I can seem to do is picture blowing him up like a hot-air balloon and watching him sail away into the sky, the same way Harry Potter did to his bitch of an aunt.

Ahhh, shit. Who am I trying to kid? I've been picturing something a little more brutal, but I've been trying to reel in my violent thoughts. It's almost Christmas. Isn't it the time of year for peace and joy? I doubt thinking about strapping my boss to the front of a car and ramming it into a brick wall is going to help me find my zen this time of year. So for now, I'll settle with the hot-air balloon.

Maybe I need to start looking into meditation. Or therapy.

Grabbing my phone, I call my best friend, Rena, and shove my phone between my ear and shoulder as I continue collecting my things off my desk, making sure to add the company stapler and scissors.

The call rings twice before Rena answers. "What's up?" my best friend's sing-song tone sails through the phone, accompanied by the sound of the busy New York streets around her.

Leaning back in my desk chair, I abandon my packing task. "It happened again," I say with a heavy sigh, feeling completely defeated.

"Ahh, shit," she mutters. "You got your period in that white pantsuit again? I swear, I told you to leave a change of clothes at the office. What do you need? Tampons and that cute outfit you bought from Zara last week? The one with the matching blazer? I'm just leaving the gym, but if you can hide out in your office, I'll be twenty minutes tops."

"What?" I grunt. "No. I didn't get my period. I got fired."

"Ooh," she says before her tone drops and she says it again. "Oooooh."

"Yeah."

The outside noises fade away, and I can only assume she's stepped into one of her favorite coffee shops on her way home. "Shit. Are you alright?" she asks.

"Yeah . . . I don't know," I tell her. "I think it's still sinking in. I love my job, but sometimes Dwayne makes it so hard to enjoy what I'm doing."

"Ugh. Dwayne is such a little asshole," she says. "I swear, that guy makes it so freaking clear that he's not getting dicked-down on the regular. I mean, why does he need to be so worked up all the time? People who fuck simply aren't that depressing to be around."

"Tell me about it."

Rena fades away as she puts in her order for a latte and a turkey sub on a whole wheat roll before coming back to me. "You know," she says, a deep thoughtfulness in her sweet tone. "You've been talking about moving on from SC Corporate for months now. Maybe this is your shot to start your own business. You're so good at what you do, but you're doing it all for a lousy paycheck at the end of the week. If you were the one calling the shots, you'd be raking it in."

"I mean . . . I thought about it, but I don't think I'm ready."

"No one is more ready than you are," she tells me. "You're literally one of the best corporate publicists in the country. Clients will flock to you. All you need is a team working under you who knows what they're doing, and then nothing will stop you."

I let out a heavy breath to suppress my hope and excitement for a dream I'm not sure I could pull off. "I don—"

"Don't even think about telling me no. This is happening," she says. "Take the Christmas break off to actually relax for once, and then start up in the new year. I'll swing by tonight and we can start hammering out all the details. I'm sure there's a bunch of licensing things you'll need, a small office space, or maybe you can work from home while you're just getting started. Oh! Then we can work out a business name and start playing with some branding options. You know that shit gets me all kinds of hot and bothered."

A grin stretches across my face, and I find myself sitting up a little straighter. "You really think I can do this?"

"You're Blair Wilder. Of course you can do this," she says. "Besides, if you're not going to do it for yourself, then do it for your nana. She was so proud of you at SC, but she would have loved to see you open your own firm."

"Shit. Don't play the nana card. That's not fair."

Rena laughs. "Never said I played fair."

"Good point," I say, rolling my eyes. "But you know as soon as the clients catch wind that I've been fired, they're going to put pressure on Dwayne to bring me back, and I—"

"No. You're going to say no and tell him where to shove his bullshit job, and when those clients get pissed that you're gone for good, they're going to leave SC Corporate Management and find you."

"You really think?"

"I know, and so do you," she says. "Now, order yourself an Uber and get your ass out of there. And do yourself a favor, go out in style. Really kick Dwayne in the balls on your way out. Make sure that when he does beg for you back, it's really going to be a shot to his ego."

A sly grin pulls at the corner of my lips. "Alright, girl. I'll see you tonight."

"That's the spirit," she says. "Talk to you later."

The call goes dead, and I put my phone back down on my desk before opening one last email. Then with a fierce courage blasting through my veins, I select the mailing list that got me into this trouble in the first place—the full company.

From: Blair Wilder - Senior Publicist, SC Corporate Management
To: All
Subject: Fired!

I'm out, Bitches!

That's right, you heard me. Dwayne did it again! Apparently yesterday's award-winning meme was deemed inappropriate, despite how those with an actual sense of humor might feel about it. Though we all know if Dwayne could take a dick as hard as he takes a joke, we wouldn't be in this position . . . again.

Anyway, this is your official heads up that I'll be starting my own PR firm in the new year, so if you're as sick of Dwayne's bullshit as I am, you know how to find me, and you know I'll look after you!

In the meantime, be sure to direct every single one of your questions and concerns to Dwayne. You know how he likes to keep busy over the Christmas period.

Have a wonderful and joy-filled Christmas with your families, and if there aren't at least a handful of scandals from out of control Christmas parties, you know I'll be disappointed.

From the boxed-up office of Blair Wilder.

I suck in a breath, and the courage that filled my veins only five minutes ago quickly begins to dwindle, but I close my eyes and hit send with quivering hands.

I suppose that's my cue to get out of here.

Grabbing what's left on my desk, I throw it into my box, and as I scoop it up, I hear the commotion starting to drum up from outside my door. A stupid grin stretches over my face, pride surging through me. I didn't exactly put Dwayne in his place in the way I've always wanted to, but it's enough to sucker punch him right in the gut, and damn it, it feels good.

Walking around my desk, I grab the spare pantsuit I keep in my cupboard for emergencies—a lesson I learned the hard way. I drop the outfits into the top of the box before grabbing my handbag and shoving it on top. Then with my box in my hands, I glance back at the office I've called home for nearly six long, rewarding years, knowing that this time, I won't be coming back.

It's time to do me. It's time to step up, grab ahold of my dreams, and make them my new reality, no matter how terrifying that might be.

Making my way back to my door, I try to juggle the box in one hand, but it's too hard, and I'm forced to bend down and catch the handle on my elbow, trying to wrestle the door open. Then just as I get a good swing on the door, Zac, the head of security, steps into my path.

"You're not serious," I say bluntly, staring at the guy who's always been a good friend to me.

"Sorry, Blair," he says, leaning toward me and taking the box out of my hands like the perfect gentleman he's always been. "I've gotta escort you out, but for what it's worth, I thought your donkey meme was fucking brilliant."

"Right," I agree. "A piece of fine art if you ask me."

Zac chuckles and nudges my door a little wider with his foot, making space for me to walk out, only I quickly double back and grab the laminator out of the cupboard. I sure as hell won't use it, but knowing it'll come out of Dwayne's monthly office budget feels fucking fantastic.

As I stride out of my office with Zac at my side, I can't help but feel dirty, like this is some kind of walk of shame, and I pick up my pace, despite not needing to feel so humiliated. These people have been my friends and colleagues for years. Most of them congratulated me on such an epic email this morning. Hell, I can even see some of them checking their latest email and chuckling to themselves. It's almost a guarantee that, at some point during their employment, every person in this office has wanted to strangle Dwayne in one way or another. He's just that much of a prick.

Some people stand and give me warm, knowing smiles, while others race into me, giving me quick hugs with a few comforting words about wanting to come with me when I start my own business. It's another ten minutes before I finally walk out the main doors of SC Corporate Management to find my Uber waiting right out front.

Zac walks with me to the Uber, easily able to juggle the heavy box with one hand to open the car door for me. "All the best, Blair," he says, giving me a fond smile. "Try not to kick too much ass. You'll make the rest of us look bad."

I can't help but laugh as I take my box from him. "Thanks, Zac," I say, the heaviness really starting to weigh down on my chest. "Have a great Christmas."

"You too," he says, and with that, I drop into my Uber, place the box and the laminator down on the seat beside me, and wonder how the hell I'm supposed to move forward from here. All I know is that from this day on, things are never going to be the same.

CHAPTER TWO
BLAIR

Dropping all of my shit on the doormat in front of my apartment, I grab my handbag out of the box and begin rifling through it for my keys. As I search the darkest pits of my handbag, I hear a strange grunting noise coming from inside my apartment, and I pause, my hand stilling inside my bag.

My brows furrow, and I hold my breath as I lean in toward my door, listening through the wood. The strange grunting sounds again, followed by a sharp smacking sound, and my eyes widen. I've got no idea what the fuck is going on in there, but I know the sound of someone being spanked when I hear it.

Grabbing the door handle, I twist, finding it already unlocked, and I throw the door open wide before storming in. My gaze quickly sweeps the living room, and I come to a startling halt, finding my boyfriend, Marc.

Tight black latex covers his whole body, right down to the leather collar locked around his throat. His dick hangs out of his fucked-up little outfit as a woman dressed in a BDSM leather harness hovers before him on her knees, a ring gag strapped around her face, forcing her mouth open.

"WHAT IN THE EVER-LOVING FUCK IS GOING ON IN HERE?" I shriek, my eyes widening in horror as I take in the guy I've been dating for the past few months. Shit, Nana tried to tell me he was a piece of shit but I defended him. I told her she just didn't know him like I did, but she was right. Nana was always right.

Marc's head snaps up, looking just as horrified as I feel. Don't get me wrong, I'm all for people exploring their kinks and being freaky little devils, but why the fuck does he have to do it in my home? As far as I'm aware, I've never given him a key, and I sure as hell have never given him the idea that he could use my home as a fucking sex chamber.

"Blair. I—"

"OUT," I demand, needing to turn away, unable to look at him. This isn't the clean-cut successful lawyer who's always gone out of his way to impress me. I don't even know the man standing before me.

"Blair, please. I can explain," he rushes out as the woman unclips the ring gag from around her mouth, clearly realizing that whatever is going on here is over.

"I don't need an explanation," I tell him, unease blasting through my veins. "I've seen enough. You broke into my apartment to live out some kind of BDSM fetish bullshit, probably thinking I'd be at work and you'd never get caught. I mean, you're a lawyer. Tell me how many laws you just broke when you stole my key and let yourself in here to fuck some bitch—no offense," I say, my gaze flicking toward the woman.

"None taken," she says with a shrug, getting to her feet. And damn it, I hate how insecure her killer body makes me feel about my own.

Keeping my attention locked on Marc, I continue. "In case you haven't worked it out, we're done. Don't ever come back here again."

"Blair—"

"OUT NOW," I roar again, taking a page out of Dwayne's book and pointing my finger toward the door as humiliation and anger burn through me like liquid rage. "Find your shit and get out of here. I don't ever want to see you again."

"But I love you."

The woman scoffs, scrunching her face at him. "Seriously? You're going to try and throw that bullshit at her? You're here in her apartment trying to fuck me. You don't love her."

Marc turns his attention to the woman as she finds her discarded shirt on my couch and pulls it on over her outfit. "Why the fuck are you still here?"

She scoffs at him. "At this point, I think I'm more welcome than you are."

"Neither of you is welcome in my home," I tell them. "Now get out before I call the police. I'm sure that would look great on your sparkly little record."

Marc clenches his jaw. "Can you at least allow me a moment to get dressed?"

"You broke into my home, Marc," I spit, not able to comprehend why the hell he's still here. "If this was a home invasion and the asshole asked for a glass of water after forcing his way into my apartment, I'd be searching for a baseball bat to beat the living shit out of him. So why the hell would you think I'd allow you that courtesy? Tuck your fucking limp dick back inside your . . . whatever the fuck you want to call that shit you're wearing and leave. Otherwise, it won't just be breaking and entering you'd be charged with, it'd be an indecent exposure charge as well. And while you're at it, take your little whore with you."

Rage boils within Marc's eyes, and he strides over to my kitchen to grab his clothes off the counter before shoving his pea-sized dick back inside his latex pants. He storms right past me, and I hope for his sake that he finds somewhere to get dressed. Otherwise, he'll have hell to pay on the streets of New York.

"I, uhhh . . . I'm still owed three hundred bucks," the woman says, still loitering in my apartment.

"That's not my problem," I tell her before waving back toward the door, signaling for her to leave before I really do have to call the police. "Your payday just walked out the door, so if you want to get your money, I suggest you go and get it, but you're not going to get it out of me."

The woman huffs before heading to the door. Only she pauses and glances back at me. "For what it's worth, if I knew this wasn't his apartment, I never would have come in. Even I can admit this is a fucked-up situation."

"You think?" I scoff.

She presses her lips into a hard line, and with that, she's gone, leaving my apartment in peace. I follow her out into the hallway before grabbing all my shit at the door and bringing it in. Then the second I can, I slam the door, making sure to deadbolt it behind me.

Letting out a heavy breath, I fall back against the locked door, my day going from bad to worse. I knew Marc was never going to be my forever. I've felt real love before, and that wasn't it. What I had with him was more like companionship, but still, I wasn't expecting that level of betrayal. I feel completely blindsided, and now, instead of spending the rest of my day sulking on my couch about losing my job, I'm going to have to disinfect my home from top to bottom.

Oh shit. What if Marc played out his kinky little games with her on my bed?

Gross. Gross. Gross.

Bile rises in my throat, and I take off down the hall, desperate to get to my bedroom. The second I race through the door, I come to a screeching stop, finding my bedroom exactly how I left it, the few decorative pillows precisely in place.

"Oh, thank God," I breathe, dropping down on the end of the bed, but I still feel icky about it anyway and immediately jump back to my feet. Just the thought of him sleeping in here with me last night has me rapidly tearing off all the blankets, sending the pillows flying across the room.

I need to spring clean this asshole out of my life.

After redressing my bed with fresh sheets, I pull my rubber dish gloves on, pulling them as far up my arms as they'll go before grabbing every cleaning product in my home and going to town on my apartment. I scrub everything, pouring bleach across the tiles until my eyeballs begin to sting, and only once every surface in my apartment is clean enough to eat off, I grab my box of things from the office and dump them out on the couch. Taking the empty box, I walk around the apartment, collecting anything of Marc's that he's left here over the past few months, then using the same tape I stole from the office, I tape up the box and shove it out into the hallway, certain I'll get around to shipping it off at some point over the next year or two.

The second the door closes behind me, peace settles through me, and I make my way over to my fridge and grab what's left of the bottle of wine I was so happily getting through yesterday, blissfully unaware of the bullshit that was waiting for me today.

Not bothering to grab a wine glass, I drink straight from the bottle, taking it with me into my bathroom before stripping out of my work clothes and running myself a bath. After adding oils and bath salts, I slip into the warm water, willing myself to relax, but honestly, until I know how I'll continue to pay the rent on my beautiful apartment and put food on my table, I don't think the word relax is going to be in my vocabulary.

Starting a business is scary at the best of times, but when there isn't money saved up to fall back on while you're trying to get off the ground, it's terrifying. I'm in a good position though. I have enough contacts to help get my business off the ground, and if I play my cards right, I could be ready to rent an office space within the first six months. Assuming I don't do something to fuck it up, of course.

But first, I'll allow myself to enjoy Christmas and New Year's.

The last time I celebrated Christmas was six years ago with Nana and Pop. Since then, my Christmases have been nothing but a quick call to my grandparents in the morning, and then spending the rest of the day buried in emails and paperwork. Hell, I don't even have a Christmas tree, and I doubt I could get a real one like we used to have back home.

Every year, Nana and Pop would drive me out to the Christmas tree farm and we'd spend hours searching for the best one. It's always been one of my most beloved traditions. Pop died the year after I left for New York, and now without Nana, I don't even know how I'm supposed to enjoy Christmas by myself. Do I bother getting a tree? Decorations? Or should I save up what little money I have left to try and give myself a little cushioning while I start up my PR firm?

But more importantly, what am I supposed to do with myself? Do I force Rena to take me in on Christmas and crash her family's traditions? I suppose I could go and offer my time down at the soup kitchen. They're always looking for helpful hands this time of year.

When my bath water starts turning my fingers into a pruney mess and no longer scalds my body, I get out and finish off what's left of my bottle of wine, knowing damn well I'm about to open a new one.

I get myself wrapped up in my winter pajamas and grab a throw blanket from the linen cupboard before snuggling up on the couch with a notepad and pen. I'm a sucker for a good list. Shopping lists. To-do lists. Skin care routine lists. Anything that could have a list, I have one for, and starting a new business is no different.

Despite Rena's plan to swing by tonight to do just this, I can't help but list off everything I need to do to get a new business up and running before making sub lists of the things I need to do to make each of those first steps happen.

Before I know it, my alarm sounds on my phone and my head snaps up, taking in the time.

6:00 p.m.

Shit.

Reaching for my phone, I silence the alarm I've kept for the past six years for every Thursday evening—my reminder to call Nana. We stuck to our tradition right until the end, and over the past month, I haven't found it in me to permanently disable the alarm. It's my final connection to Nana, the one thing nobody could ever take away from me.

God, I loved her so much. It's still crazy to think she's really gone, but that's the thing about distance, it warps reality. When you see somebody every day and suddenly they're gone, you notice their absence in a way long-distance relationships simply don't. I have to keep reminding myself that she's gone, but if I was back home in Blushing, I would feel it every day in the silence of our home, the coldness of floors beneath my feet, in the way the fresh aroma of coffee would fill the house first thing in the morning.

She was my everything. Right from the day my mother abandoned me and left me all alone on Nana's doorstep, crying for her to come back. I was only six, and I still haven't been able to forgive her. But Nana and Pop gave me the life she never would have been capable of and for that, I'm grateful.

I'm just putting my phone back down on the armrest of my couch when a knock sounds at the door and my brows furrow. I haven't ordered any food and Rena isn't due to be here for another two hours.

Throwing my blanket back, I get up and trudge over to the door, pulling it open a moment later to find a courier with an A4 envelope waiting in his hand. Considering he didn't have the access code to the main entrance of the apartment complex, he shouldn't have been able to get to my door.

"Are you Blair Wilder?" he mutters, clearly not very enthusiastic about his job.

"Yes," I respond, my brows furrowing just a little bit more.

He shoves the envelope into my hand before offering me a little tablet. "Sign here."

My gaze sails to the front of the envelope, reading the branding at the top—Roderick Associates & Co. My stomach drops.

Shit.

Dwayne's gone and hired a lawyer. I bet he's spent his whole afternoon scrambling through client contracts, making sure there's a solid non-compete clause so that I can't poach the firm's clients.

"What's this?" I ask the courier, hesitating to sign on the device.

"I don't know, ma'am. That's your business, not mine," he says in a flat, monotone voice, probably dying to get out of here so that he can finish his rounds and get home.

"Shit," I sigh before quickly scribbling my signature onto the tablet.

I hand it back and he takes it with a subtle nod before disappearing from my front door. Closing the door, I trudge back to the couch and flip the envelope over to slide my finger beneath the sealed tab. As I work my finger across the opening, my stomach flip flops, certain I'm about to get hit with some bullshit defamation case.

Dropping my ass to the couch, I abandon the blanket, too worked up for comfort, and I slip my hand inside to collect the papers. Only it's not what I thought, not even close.

My gaze trails over the cover letter.

Dear Miss Blair Wilder,

Please accept this letter from your beloved nana, Mrs. Olivia Grace Wilder, in which was left in her will. If you have any questions or concerns, please don't hesitate to call.

Mrs. Wilder has assured me that all instructions have been left in the attached letter.

Benjamin Roderick
Roderick Associates & Co.

My heart races, and as I flip the page over to reveal the handwritten letter from my nana, I become overwhelmed with the grief of losing her. Tears fill my eyes, and despite the way they make the papers blurry before me, I do my best to read through them, desperate for any shred of her I can get.

My sweet girl,

Quit crying! You're going to mess up the paper, and I've worked too hard trying to figure out what I want to say here for you to mess it up. Head up. You're too strong for tears, always have been.

If you're reading this, it means I'm gone. How cheesy is that? It's such a movie line, but yet, I find myself incapable of figuring out a better opener, so for now, I'll stick with the cheesy stuff. Something tells me you won't mind though.

Assuming I picked a reliable lawyer to handle my will, you should be receiving this letter at 6 p.m. on Thursday night, a month following my passing. I figured why not have one last hurrah and keep my long-standing appointment? After all, I know how you like to keep on schedule!

First and foremost, my sweet Blair, I want you to know that you're going to be just fine, and despite those nasty thoughts I know are circling your mind, you're not alone in this big world. You have created such a wonderful life for yourself over there in New York, and I am so unbelievably proud of you. You set out to conquer the world, and that's exactly what you're doing, though I know this is only the beginning for you. You still have so much more to conquer.

I want so much for you. Unbreakable and honest friendships that will last through the ages. Undeniable joy and happiness. I want you to experience the wonders of becoming a mother and learning what it means to love your child unconditionally. There truly isn't anything like it. However, first, I want you to open your heart to love the same way I did with your grandfather. I would love nothing more than for you to experience the wonders of love and to discover just how deep it can run, because one day when your babies have grown and left the nest, you're going to look around, and right there by your side, he will be there, waiting to experience a whole new adventure with you.

I know that's a lot to ask. That opening your heart like that can be scary, but I have faith in you, Blair. When the time is right, you'll find exactly what you've always been searching for, and I can't wait to watch over you as you fall in love and experience it all, just as I did at eighteen. But just remember, your pop is watching over you too, so let's keep it classy, Sweetheart. He's already suffered one fatal heart attack. He doesn't need to find out what one is like in the afterlife.

Now, on to the important stuff.

In the bottom of the envelope, you will find the key to my home—my home that is now yours.

If anybody deserves it, it's you.

By now, the deeds to my home should have already been transferred into your name, and it is completely up to you as to what you would like to do with it. Keep or sell, it's your decision. Your grandfather and I spoke at length about this before his passing, and we both agreed that there would be no hard feelings if you wanted to sell our family home.

You have a life in New York, and you have always talked about taking on such admirable dreams. I know the funds from selling the house could go far in helping those dreams come true. However, if you choose to move back to Blushing and make our home yours once again, then please, if it's the last thing you do, look after my garden. I spent way too many hours on that!

Despite how you deny it, I know the idea of returning to Blushing has always terrified you, but you need to remember that the little girl I raised and watched grow into a miraculous young woman is capable of facing anything. That little girl is strong and courageous. She always wanted to face the world with her head held high, and I know that's exactly what you're going to do.

Now, wipe those tears. You're getting snot everywhere.

I love you to the moon and back, and until the day we meet again, know that I am always watching over you, always blessing your day, and always wishing the best for every adventure you embark upon.

I look forward to the day I get to hold you in my arms again, but until then, live your best life, my darling girl. Conquer the world just as I always knew you would.

Your Nana.

xxx

What in the ever-loving fuck? Her house?

She left me her house?

Holy shit! What am I supposed to do with a house all the way over in Blushing, Colorado?

I wipe the back of my arm across my face, mop up the tears, and laugh over just how well my nana always knew me. Right down to getting snot everywhere. Then before I can even come up with a plan or begin a new list, my gaze lifts back to the letter, and I read it over and over again.

A house. I just inherited a whole damn house. That's insane.

I'm not going to lie, after Nana passed, I had wondered what was going to happen to her estate, but when nothing came, I had assumed she had organized other plans, but me? This is crazy.

The house I grew up in is absolutely beautiful. It's modest and homey with beautifully tended gardens, and while the thought of selling it makes something ache in my chest, there's no denying that this came at the perfect time.

I need funds to support me while I build this new business. Hell, I need funds just to be able to afford my rent, water, food, and power. I can hardly build a business if I can't look after myself first and foremost. Don't get me wrong, I have enough cash to get through a month or two, but what about after that? Where does that leave me? Fuck Dwayne and his shitty timing. I needed that Christmas bonus.

Shit. Am I really considering selling Nana's home? The place where all of my childhood memories are? The place I learned how to ride a bike, and where Pop taught me how to make snow angels? But do I really have any other choice?

I could sell the property over the next few weeks and close right before I open my new business. It's short notice, but it's not as though I have anything else going on right now. My now ex-boyfriend likes to dress up in latex and spank random women with ring gags, and it's not as though I have an office I need to be in right now.

I have nothing but time on my hands. Is this some kind of gift from above? Has Nana been watching over me today and knew just how much I needed this?

There's only one problem though. If I'm going to sell Nana's property, I have to go back to Blushing. I need to make sure the house is suitable for sale and bring it back into this century, but in order to do that, I'm going to have to face everything I've worked my ass off to avoid.

Nicholas Stone.

What could possibly go wrong?

CHAPTER THREE
BLAIR

Oh God! What was I thinking?

The plane touched down in Denver, Colorado two hours ago, and after catching another connecting flight to the Yampa Valley Regional Airport, I'm one step closer to returning to the one place I've truly felt was home.

The small airplane taxis back toward the terminal, and with every passing second, my heart races just a little bit more. Blushing is roughly another hour's drive from here. It's a sweet, secluded small town that has always given me Gilmore Girls vibes. Hell, Nana and I always joked that we could have easily been cast in that show. Only, she didn't fancy the idea of playing Lorelai. She was too loved-up with Pop to consider the single, struggling mom life. That was until Lorelai started dating Luke of course.

We used to watch that show religiously, just something special we would do together while Pop rolled his eyes and muttered about not understanding the show's humor.

My head aches after spending the main trip from New York into Denver getting drunk and spilling my guts to the poor, undeserving gentleman beside me. I told him my whole life story, told him all about Nick and how he was my whole world, and how I gave it all up to follow my dreams. I told him about Nana, then bitched about Dwayne and his stupid salmon button-down shirt, then about my grand plan to start up my own business after selling Nana's property over Christmas.

I'm not usually one to talk to a complete stranger like that, and if it weren't for the fact that I was on a plane, I'm sure I would have been fine. Air travel has a way of making me anxious, and if it were a longer flight, I would have taken a pill and knocked myself out for the duration of it, but unfortunately, I wasn't that lucky. So, instead of being relaxed after spending the day sleeping off the anxiety, I now find myself pissed off with a killer headache and still struggling with the anxiety of returning home.

It's another twenty minutes before I'm at baggage claim to collect my suitcase off the small carousel, and honestly, despite the multiple lists and planning I've done over the last two days, I have no idea what I'm supposed to do from here. There's not exactly a taxi bay or a million Ubers waiting around to take me back to Blushing. Don't get me wrong, I certainly tried to hire a driver and figure something out, but from the looks of it, the one driver I did manage to book has clearly bailed.

Shit.

Even during all my college traveling, I never really had this issue. Pop was always here when I landed to give me a ride. Now I have to fend for myself.

Letting out a heavy sigh, I make my way out into the chilly December air, cringing as I take in the snow-covered landscape. Don't get me wrong, New York can be bitterly cold this time of year, but my collection of cute ankle boots, heels, and athletic shoes is not cut out for the knee-deep snow here in Blushing.

My gaze sweeps up and down, trying to figure something out, and after realizing just how alone I am, I scurry back inside and park my ass on a small bench. My thin wool peacoat isn't going to cut it, so I pull it off and scramble through my suitcase. I pull out an old sweater and shrug it on over my head. It doesn't exactly match my outfit, but layering my coat over top of it will be much warmer.

The bite in the harsh breeze outside warns me that we might be in for a storm tonight, and I pull my phone out of my handbag, scrounging through my contact list trying to figure out how to get my ass home. It's been over a month since anyone has entered that house. I'm not even sure if it still has electricity or running water.

Scrolling past my high school best friend, Sarah, my thumb pauses. I haven't spoken to her in years, but she's the kind of person who would have dropped everything to help someone out. Guilt soars through my veins, but desperate times call for desperate measures, and I press her name before shoving the phone against my cold ear.

The phone rings three times before I hear Sarah's hesitant voice coming through my small speaker. "Hello?" she says as though asking a question, probably certain that I've pocket-dialed her.

"Hey, Sarah. It's Blair Wilder. How are you?" I say, trying to sound chirpy despite my current situation.

"Oh, hey," she replies. "It's been ages since we've talked. I'm doing really well. What about you?"

"That's uhhh . . . that's why I called," I say with a cringe. "I'm so sorry to dump this on you like this, but I'm kind of in a tricky situation. I've just flown in, and I'm stranded at the airport. My driver bailed, and I can't seem to order an Uber. Is there any way you'd be able to help me out? I'd absolutely pay you back."

"Oh shit, Blair. I'm so sorry. I'm actually working as a nurse now, and I'm on shift at the hospital, but give me a minute. I have a friend who works out that way and he should be finishing work around now. I'll see if he can swing by and grab you."

"Oh my God. Thank you so much," I say, letting out a heavy sigh of relief. "You have no idea how much that would save my ass right now."

"Trust me, I know. It looks like we're in for a storm tonight, and the last thing you need is to be stranded at an airport, or worse, stranded on the highway somewhere."

"You've got that right."

Sarah chuckles a small laugh. "Plus, I'd really prefer not to end my night having to admit you as a patient. I'd rather catch up over coffee instead."

"Consider it a date," I say as my first real smile in days spreads across my face.

"Okay, give me a minute. I'll call Oxley and see if he can grab you," she says as my mind begins to swirl. Oxley? Why is there something so familiar about that name? It sits right in the forefront of my brain, waiting to be plucked out and formed into existence, but before I can think about it anymore, Sarah continues. "I'll text you in a minute and let you know what he says."

The relief is so great that all thoughts of familiarity fall away, and all that matters is the idea that I might just get back to Blushing before the storm hits. "Thanks, Sarah. I owe you one."

"You absolutely do not," she says, and with that, the call goes dead.

Letting out a heavy sigh, I settle into my seat, trying to get comfortable, but the hard bench isn't doing my ass any favors, especially after being stuck on planes for the majority of my afternoon. It's only a minute before my phone beeps with an incoming text and I glance down, smiling at Sarah's name as it appears on my screen.

Sarah - Good timing. Ox is only five minutes away. He said he can grab you. He's in a blue pickup, pretty boy, most likely wearing his cap backwards because he thinks he's hot like that!

Relief pounds through my veins, and I quickly respond.

Blair - You are a life saver!!!!!! Text me when you're free and we'll catch up.

Sarah - Will do. I'm really happy you're back. I've missed you.

Blair - Missed you too. Xx

Thank God. I don't know what I would have done if she hadn't come to the rescue. Most of the people I knew from here so long ago have probably moved on and started their own lives in new towns with their babies and partners. The only other person I know who is still here . . . well, he's not an option. Hell, I only know he's still in Blushing because Nana would mention it every now and then in the hopes that I would see the errors of my ways and race back here to rekindle young love. She always wanted to see me get married and start a family, but I'm pretty sure she would have tempted me with anything just to get me back home.

Just as Sarah said, it's only a quick five minutes before a tall blonde with scruffy hair under his backward cap waltzes through the front door, looking more than a little lost. He wears an old flannel button-down with the sleeves rolled up as though he hasn't noticed the mounds of freezing snow.

His head sweeps from left to right, and I can't help but trail my greedy gaze over him. He's a farm boy through and through, and damnnnnn, it looks good on him . . . or maybe I've just been deprived of what a real farm boy looks like for so long.

I almost start drooling.

I grew up ogling guys like Oxley until I set my sights on Nick. They simply don't grow them this way in New York. I've become accustomed to arrogant men in fancy tailored suits, but I won't find a single designer brand out here in Blushing. People here are so chilled out. They don't care about wasting their hard-earned dollars on expensive things when they could use that money to go out and have a good time, spoil their friends, and treat their families.

Not wanting to risk Oxley walking away, I quickly stand and grab my bag before scurrying across the foyer of the airport. "Are you Oxley?" I ask as I approach him, despite already being ninety-nine percent sure.

His blue-gray eyes swivel to me as a grin lifts the corner of his lips. "That'll be me, sweetheart," he says with a slight drawl to his tone, something I haven't heard in so long. His gaze sweeps over me, taking in my tight jeans, coat, and ankle boots, clearly able to tell that I'm a city girl. "You must be Blair."

"I am," I say, holding out my hand toward him. He gives it a quick shake, and I offer him a beaming smile as my hand falls away. "Thank you so much for picking me up."

"No problem," he says, nodding his head toward the door, indicating for me to get my ass moving. I fall in line beside him, and he slips his hand over mine, taking my suitcase like the perfect gentleman. "Trust me. When Sarah calls and asks for a favor, it's in your best interest to make it happen."

I laugh, loving that she's still the same Sarah I've always known and loved. "It's good to see that some things never change."

We reach his blue pickup, and he lifts my suitcase into the bed of the truck as his blue-gray gaze sweeps toward me. "Oh, you're from around here?" he asks, his brows furrowing as though trying to place me.

"Yeah, I grew up here," I explain as I open the door and climb into the warmth of his pickup. He gets in the driver's seat and quickly kicks over the engine, and the whole truck vibrates to life just like my pop's used to do. "I went to Blushing High, but once I started college, I wasn't around much after that. I flew back home as much as I could, but that wasn't always easy."

"I can imagine," he says, hitting the road and sending us flying back toward the home I've avoided for so long. "So, you're coming home to be with your family over the Christmas break?"

I take a breath, not really sure if I can talk about it, but there's no point in lying. Blushing is a small town, and he'll figure it out sooner or later. "Not exactly," I tell him as my chest tightens. "My nana passed away a few weeks ago, and I'm all she had left. So I'm coming home to sort out her estate."

"Ahh, shit. I'm sorry," he says. "My aunt passed a few months ago, and my cousin and I were left to do the same thing. It's rough."

"Tell me about it," I mutter. "I'm terrified to walk back into that house and not see her sitting in her old rocking chair, knitting something for her future great grandchildren while screaming at the TV."

"Yeah, I bet. The first time is going to suck. I won't sugarcoat it," he says, sparing me a quick glance as the snowfall picks up, getting a little heavier. "But once you get in there and the grief begins to settle, you'll start thinking about the good times, and it won't be so hard."

"I really hope so."

"What about you?" I ask. "Any extravagant plans for the holiday break?"

"Nah. Just chilling at home with the boyfriend," he says as disappointment clutches onto me like a bad rash. Shit. He's got a boyfriend. Why the hell didn't I see that coming? "I, uhhh . . . can you keep a secret?"

"Ohhhh, a secret?" I ask, chirping right back up. "I love a good secret."

"But can you keep them?" Oxley prompts.

I make a show of zipping my lips and locking them with a key. "Best secret keeper in town," I promise.

Oxley eyes me warily, studying me a little too closely for comfort before clearly deciding he can trust me. He reaches over to my side of the truck and opens the glove box in front of my knees. Then while keeping his eyes locked on the snowy road, he feels around inside the glove box before finally pulling out a small velvet box.

"Check it out," he says, handing me the box.

My brows furrow, my heart already racing for what I think is inside, and I slowly open it, finding a silver engagement band. A wide smile spreads across my face. "HOLY SHIT!" I screech. "You're proposing?"

Oxley grins right back and nods. "That's the plan," he says. "I'm hoping to pop the question on Christmas. Or maybe Christmas Eve. I haven't really decided yet."

"Oooh, Christmas Eve would be nice. You could do a romantic

candlelit dinner and then you have all of Christmas Day to share it with your families, and then you won't need to spend all of Christmas Day shitting yourself with nerves."

"That's a very good point," he says before launching into the many ideas he's had and asking every bit of advice—not that I'm really the right person to be asking. Apart from Nick, the only real romance I've ever experienced is in movies and books.

We're just driving past the big Welcome to Blushing sign when Oxley glances back at me. "Where am I dropping you?"

"Do you know the old Wilder place?" I ask rather than giving a physical address because as a general rule, everybody knows everybody around here, and if they don't, they're new.

"Sure do. I've had my ass handed to me by Olivia on more than enough—wait," he says, swinging his stare back to me, his brows arched with curiosity. "You're that Blair? Olivia's granddaughter who took off to the big city. The Blair I used to hear about every time she faked a plumbing issue just to get someone over to her place so she could cook a meal and eat with someone?"

A fond smile spreads across my face at the same time a pang of guilt slices through me, realizing just how lonely she was. "Yep. That'll be me," I mutter, able to picture everything he just said so perfectly.

"Shit," he laughs, smiling as though he knows something he shouldn't. "You're kinda famous around these parts."

"Oh God. I can only imagine what Nana has said about me over the years."

"Nah, it was all good," Oxley tells me, mirroring that same fond smile that was on my face only a moment ago. "You were the apple of her eye, and apparently the apple of someone else's eye."

Jesus. I forgot how quickly word travels in a small town. I suppose everyone knows my business.

My stomach sinks, knowing exactly who he's referring to, and all I can do is offer a tight smile before glancing back out the window and watching Oxley navigate the familiar roads that I used to spend days on end running through. I suck in a breath, cringing as I peek back at him. "You know him?"

"Who doesn't?"

"Good point," I say in a small voice. "But for the record, I'm . . . I'm not here for him."

"Uh-huh," he grins, the tension beginning to fill the truck.

"Really. I'm not. I just want to check out what state Nana's house is in, put it up for sale, and get my ass back to New York," I admit as we pass the local fruit market, and the grocery store on the corner. We pass Julie's Dance School and then the elementary school that I absolutely hated. "Besides, I'm sure the last thing Nick wants is to see the girl who broke his heart all those years ago. He's amazing and gorgeous, and I wouldn't be surprised if some lucky woman scooped him up the minute she could."

"Not gonna lie, there's more than a few girls who've always had their eye on him, but none of them really seem to hold his attention."

"Wait. So he's—"

"Still single?" he questions, his brow arching once again.

I shake my head. I don't need to know the answer to that, and

I definitely don't need the temptation—not that Nick would want anything to do with me after the way I left things. God, I'm sure he hates me for breaking his heart like that. The best thing for me to do is to stay holed up in Nana's house, not disturb the peace, and get out of here as soon as I can.

Oxley turns down Nana's street, and I find myself sitting up in my seat, my eyes wide as the memories crash over me in waves. Learning to ride my bike with Pop. Gardening with Nana. Sneaking out my bedroom window for the first time while Nick waited down the street for me.

God. I always loved it here.

Oxley parks along the curb, not bothering to pull into the snow-covered driveway. "Here," he says, pulling out a small business card and scrawling his number on the back. "Call me if you need anything while you're here. Or if you just need a little company."

"Thanks, Oxley," I say, taking the card from him and sliding it into my handbag. "I owe you."

"Just Ox," he says with a nod.

He gets out to help me with my suitcase, and a moment later, I'm standing at the end of the driveway, staring up at the beautiful cottage.

"I'll take a shot in the dark and assume I'll be seeing you around," Ox says, striding back to his driver's door as I palm the front door key in my hand, turning it over and over as though too scared to actually use it.

"For some reason, I don't doubt that," I tell him, feeling as though I just made what could possibly be a really great friend. And with that, Ox hops into his truck and takes off, leaving me to face this all alone.

CHAPTER FOUR
NICK

Leaning over the new storage shelf at Hardin's Hardware, I tighten the final bolt before stepping back and surveying my handiwork. Pretty fucking good if you ask me.

Not going to lie, building a shelf for a hardware store isn't exactly what I had planned for my day, but when you have a particular set of skills in a small town, you quickly turn into the local maintenance and handyman. I don't mind it though.

People who know me well will usually call me directly and hire me for a job, but those who don't exactly appreciate my less-than-friendly demeanor tend to call the hardware store, hoping John could help them out. But it's unlikely, and lately, those jobs have been coming straight to me too. Can't complain, I like money.

John Hardin has been running the hardware store since before I can remember. It's been in his family for six generations—a fact he's always sure to remind me of—and if he had found the time to start a family of his own when he was younger, I'm sure he'd have a middle-aged son here doing this for him and demanding he quit being such a stubborn ass and retire already. But it's never going to happen, John will be here until he physically can't get up in the morning. Hell, I don't think in the last fifty or so years he's even taken a day off.

A few years ago, John would have told me to fuck off and insisted that he could put the shelf together himself, but lately, things are starting to slip. He doesn't have the strength in his hands to work the way he used to, and when stock started piling up on the ground, creating hazards for him out in the back storage area, I couldn't take it anymore and ordered the stubborn asshole a new set of shelves. Someone's got to look after him, right?

As I grab boxes of stock and shove them onto the new shelves to tidy up the mess around me, I hear the familiar chimes of the bell over the door of the hardware store. Shuffling footsteps move through the store, shifting across the old wooden floorboards before a familiar tone cuts through the silence. "Nick out back?" I hear my cousin ask.

"Being a menace, as usual," John mutters in response.

Oxley laughs, and as I continue stacking shelves, I hear him creep through the store until the footsteps are right at my back.

Glancing over my shoulder, I find Ox leaning against the doorframe of the storage room, his gaze shifting around at the mess at my feet. "Fuck me," he grumbles, pulling off his backward cap and running his fingers through his untamed hair. "It's a mess in here."

"Why do you think I'm back here? Knowing John, he'll probably fall and break a hip, only to tell his hip to harden the fuck up and keep working through the pain."

Ox laughs, a smirk playing on his lips. He knows I'm right. "Fuck. He's a stubborn bastard." Ox shifts nervously from one foot to another, and my brows furrow, pausing as I hover over the next box. It's not unusual for him to spot my truck around town and stop to say hello, but it sure as fuck is unusual for him to hover nervously. He's not the kind to mince his words. If something's on his mind, he says it. He doesn't give a shit about someone else's opinion. But this right here, this isn't him.

Something's going on.

"Spit it out," I grunt, scooping up the next box and shoving it onto the shelf, doing what I can to keep everything in order, but let's be honest, John will be back here the second I leave to reorganize every single shelf.

Ox cringes, and his hesitation only pisses me off. I'm not the kind to give a shit about other people's lives. Their drama and bullshit doesn't interest me. Hell, people in general don't interest me, but for some reason unknown to me, Oxley does. He's been a pain in my ass my whole life, and after my mom passed a few months ago, he's made it his personal mission to check in on me every fucking day.

Don't get me wrong, I love the asshole, but not that much. Oxley Stone is an acquired taste.

"You have two fucking seconds to say what you've gotta say," I murmur, knowing damn well he'll take my warning seriously. After all, we grew up together, and he knows I don't fuck around. If you want to piss me off, you'll find your head shoved through the drywall. Oxley has always joked that I'm the definition of fuck around and find out. Though, I've certainly mellowed from those reckless teen years. There was one person, one reason that pushed me to be better. I wanted to be her everything. I wanted to be the reason for the smile on her face every fucking day, and then she was gone, and I was left with a gaping hole right through the center of my chest. It's a wound that's never been able to heal. No matter how hard I try, nothing has been able to mend the hollowness inside of me. So instead, I live my life just like John, two kindred spirits barely making it through the day.

Oxley inches toward me, fixing his cap back onto his head. He lets out a subtle sigh, his only indication that he's trying his hardest to be gentle with whatever bomb is about to fly out of his mouth. "She's back, man."

My back stiffens, my heart thundering wildly in my chest.

He doesn't need to tell me who she is. I already know. The whole fucking town knows about the girl who tore my heart to shreds because I've never been the same. We were the town's it couple. Hell, even at sixteen, only a few short months after officially becoming an item, we had Bessy from Blushing's grocery market and Julie who runs the town's dance school planning our eventual wedding.

Blair fucking Wilder—the ghost who will forever haunt me.

She can't be back.

Keeping my gaze locked on the box, I shove it onto the shelf, holding my back toward Oxley, not wanting him to see how the blood has drained from my face or the way my fingers have dug into the side of the cardboard. "So?"

"So?" he scoffs, and I can imagine the way his eyes bulge out of his head. "She's back. Blair is in Blushing, just down the fucking road in that old cottage of her nana's, and after the past six years of pining for her, that's your response?"

I shrug, trying to hide the agony ripping through my chest. "What did you hope I'd say? That I'd run over there and beg on my knees for her to take me back?" I bend down and grab another box, shoving it onto the shelf with far too much enthusiasm that I hear the contents inside rattling around. "She left six years ago without a single fucking thought for the people she left behind and hasn't been back since. She's not interested in having me walk back into her life, and in case you haven't figured it out, I'm not interested in having her chew me up and spit me out again."

Oxley scoffs, crossing his arms over his chest before leaning back against the drywall. "You're not even going to pretend to care?"

"Don't see why I should."

He shakes his head, and I feel the judgment wafting off him in waves. "You know why she's here, right?" he questions.

I roll my eyes, grabbing another box. Of course I know why she's here. Does he think I'm a fucking idiot? Hell, I've been expecting her to come waltzing back into town sooner or later, and honestly, considering it's already been a month since Olivia passed, I'm disappointed. Blair didn't even make the effort to fly in for her funeral. But that leaves

Olivia's estate, and assuming there's nothing else in this small town to entice her to return home, I can only assume that's why she's here.

The question is, how the fuck does Oxley know?

I turn my gaze on his blue eyes, eyes so similar to mine that it messes with my head sometimes. Hell, we could be brothers . . . if he wasn't such a pretty boy, of course. "Of course I know why she's here," I mutter. "But how the fuck do you know?"

I know Blushing is a small town and all, but it's not small enough that everyone shits in each other's pockets. Oxley knows of Blair through me, and while I've made an effort to look out for Olivia these past few years, especially after Blair's pop died, Oxley never really had much to do with her. Though the handful of times they spoke, Olivia wouldn't be able to stop bragging about her hotshot granddaughter living out in the big city and conquering the world.

"I, uhhh . . ." A sheepish expression crosses his face, and as he cringes, I narrow my stare in silent warning. "I got a call from Sarah. She said a friend was stranded at the airport and needed a lift back into town. I was close by so of course I picked her up, and it wasn't until we were halfway back to Blushing that I realized who she was."

Clenching my jaw, I nod before letting my gaze fall back to the boxes, and it seems the more information he relays, the harder my heart booms in my chest. "So, she's only here for a little while, then?"

Oxley shrugs his shoulders. "I don't think she's thought that far," he says, and I quickly realize it was the wrong question to ask because the second the words come out of his mouth, a small beam of hope pulses in the pit of my stomach—a beam of hope that I need to crush as soon as I can.

"Cool," I murmur, feigning indifference, but fuck, I know he doesn't buy it. Apart from Blair, Ox is the only other person who's ever been able to read me.

"Uh-huh," he says, choosing not to call me out on my bullshit as he picks an invisible piece of lint from his stupid flannel jacket. "I just figured I'd warn you instead of letting you get blindsided when you inevitably run into her in town. You know, because we both know if that happened, you'd stand there gawking at her like a fucking idiot. But now that you know, you can practice your pleasantly surprised reaction in the mirror like a normal hung-up loser."

"I'm not hung up on her."

"Uh-huh. And I'm not my mother's greatest disappointment," he says, trying to make some stupid point. "Look, I've gotta go, but do yourself a favor and go say hi. Who knows? There might just be something still there worth exploring. And if not, you might just get the answers to the questions you've been needing to ask for six long years. Hell, you might even get the closure you've needed to move on."

I scoff and shove another box onto the shelf. He couldn't be more wrong.

Me move on from Blair Wilder? Fucking impossible. I'd have better luck trying to shoot myself into outer space using a slingshot and a homemade propeller. But he's right about one thing—I have a shitload of unanswered questions, and every one of them revolves around how the hell she could walk away so easily.

Ox makes his way toward the door and pauses, glancing back and demanding my attention. "She looked fucking good, Nick," he tells me. "Gorgeous. You'd be a fool not to at least try."

With those parting words, he's gone, leaving me to stew in a world of self-destruction. I finish stacking all the boxes in easy-to-manage rows for when John inevitably rearranges everything late tonight. I'll have to be sure to stop by in the morning just to make sure he doesn't need a damn ambulance.

After striding out of Hardin's Hardware, I drop my toolbox into the bed of my red pickup before driving myself home. It's fucking lonely here. I bought this property for me and Blair back when she was in her final year of college. It was going to be a surprise, our chance to start our lives together and build a home for us to raise a family, but she was gone before I could even tell her about it.

I still went ahead and built a home—a fucking brilliant one if you ask me—but it's always been tainted by the ghost of her. Of what could have been, what should have been.

It took nearly four years to build, but the two-story modern farmhouse home is everything I dreamed it could be. I live on the outskirts of town with enough property to do whatever the hell I want. High ceilings, open living space, a roaring fireplace with a wraparound porch so I can take in the expansive view from every corner of my home. But no matter how beautiful or elegant it is, it doesn't change the fact that it's the loneliest house in Blushing.

After getting myself fed and showered after a long day, I find myself sitting out on my deck, my gaze locked on the snow-covered hills in the distance, the moonlight barely casting enough of a glow to see. During the day, I'd be able to see the lake that runs along the border of my property. It's frozen solid by now, and if I were the kind to care about the usual Christmas traditions, I'd have figured out how to smooth it out and break out my old hockey skates from high school.

My knee bounces, and it's impossible to keep still.

Ever since Ox muttered those two words, I've been a mess. She's back.

Blair Wilder is back, and I don't know how to feel about it. I don't even know how to keep myself from thinking about it. She's been back all of two seconds, and I'm already a wreck.

I need to know how long she intends to be here. So I can put this raging ache to rest. The sooner I can start pretending that she isn't just down the road, the sooner life can get back to normal.

Tomorrow. Tomorrow is the day I'll get my answers. I'll man up, head over there, and demand to know what the fuck she's doing back in my town, and after that . . . I haven't got a clue. Probably search for solace at the bottom of a bottle of Jack.

Fucking hell. Oxley was right. I'm hung up on Blair Wilder. So fucking hung up that I throw myself out of my deck chair and storm in through the back door of my home, and before I even know what I'm doing, I'm flying out the front door and crashing into the driver's side of my red pickup.

The engine roars to life, and within the space of only a few minutes, I'm already sailing through the middle of town. I detour, taking the long way around to avoid going past Oxley's place because, without a doubt, he'll know exactly what I'm doing, and I'll surely receive a call telling me to turn my ass right around.

Turning down the familiar street, I roll to a stop in front of the neighbor's home. I don't exactly get the best view from here, but it's enough to get my first glimpse of the woman who tore me to shreds.

She stands in the living room with long brunette hair cascading down her back, piling small logs into the old fireplace. She looks different than when I saw her last. She was so full of life six years ago, so ready to claim everything she's always wanted, but the woman I see through the window is dejected. Clouded by grief. Her shoulders sag forward, almost slouching, and while it's been a long time since I've seen her, I could almost swear that she's lost weight.

If only she would turn around and gaze out the window. I need to see those bright blue eyes, need to get a good read on her just to know that she's alright.

My heart races as my feelings get caught in my throat. She's so fucking beautiful. Always has been. I've wondered what she'd look like now, wondered what she'd think of the man I've become . . . fuck. Do I even hear myself? I sound like a fucking love-sick puppy who can't catch a hint.

She doesn't want me, and I'm sure the last thing she wonders about is the lost cause she walked away from six years ago.

Blair reaches up over the fireplace, and I watch as she curls her hand around a lighter before crouching down and doing her best to light the wood, but it's clear she hasn't got a single fucking clue what she's doing. Her pop was always in charge of putting the fire on, a real man's man who looked after his girls. He never made them lift a finger for fear they might hurt themselves.

Over in her cushy life in New York, I'm sure Blair's little apartment doesn't boast a fireplace, and I can only imagine that right now as she struggles with the cold, she's desperate to get back home to her thermostat.

She gives up after ten minutes of struggling before digging out the old electric heater, and I cringe. That thing is a fire hazard in itself, probably bought a million years ago. She'd be safer with a controlled fire. But I suppose that's none of my business.

Blair drags the old heater across the living room and disappears out of sight, and as I wait for her return, my gaze lingers on the property. The driveway is covered in snow, at least knee high, and the roof has inches of snow piled on top.

The driveway is an issue, but for now, the roof will be alright. As for the few icicles hanging from the gutters, they've got to go.

I clench my jaw, my hand tightening around the steering wheel as I start repeating my new mantra—She's not my problem. She's not my problem.

As if on cue, the lights go out in the old cottage, and I let out a relieved breath, feeling as though I've somehow gotten away with something. I can no longer see through the window, and after sitting out here for another twenty minutes convinced that she's gone to bed, my hand hesitates over the shifter.

If she walked out first thing in the morning and one of those icicles fell down and injured her, I'd never be able to forgive myself.

"Fuck," I mutter, letting out another heavy breath.

Opening my door, I push through to the cold night, leaving my truck running, and hurry up the slick sidewalk, following the footprints she's already made in the snow. Walking up to the front door, a sense of déjà vu floods through me, remembering the million times I've walked up to this very door and knocked on it, asking Blair's pop if I could take her out for dinner. He always got a kick out of forcing me to be a chivalrous asshat, but I really didn't mind it, especially when it put a wide smile on Blair's face.

Standing on the porch, I quickly get to work, removing the icicles and freezing my hand in the process. I'm sure there's more out back, but for now, clearing the ones off the front will have to do. I toss the icicles into the back portion of the garden, making sure they're far enough back that Blair won't accidentally step on them.

When the last of them are gone, I wipe my cold hands on my pants, and as I go to take off back toward my truck before I manage to wake her, my gaze settles on the snow-filled driveway. It really is dangerous. There could be ice under this snow, and one misstep could—not my problem. She's not my problem.

Fuck.

Shifting my stance, I blow my cheeks out and make my way around the back of the property. The shed doors stand slightly ajar, and I find the snow shovel right where I left it last season. After Blair's pop died, I took on looking after Olivia. She didn't have any other family left in Blushing, and she blatantly refused to move out to New York to be with Blair. This was her home, and despite how much she loved Blair, nothing could get her out of it.

My fingers curl around the shovel, and before I know it, I'm standing at the top of the porch and getting started on the snow piled high on the pavement. The sidewalk takes a good twenty minutes to clear, and I follow it down until I reach the top of the driveway.

God. I'm such a fucking sucker. At least the storm we were supposed to get seems to have passed over us and all of this effort won't be for nothing. Though there's no denying that she will know I've been here now. At least, I think she will. Who knows. I guess I don't really know her anymore. She's a complete mystery to me now.

After spending an hour on the driveway clearing weeks' worth of snow, I put the shovel back in the shed before doing a quick check of the property and making sure none of the garden hoses had exploded from the sheer pressure of the ice within.

There are a few more icicles around the back, and I quickly knock them off. Then before I can convince myself to break through the side window and cut the power to the old fire risk of a heater, I force myself down the cleared driveway and back into the warmth of my truck.

Content that she won't break an ankle, I hit the gas and sail back across town, desperately wishing that things could have been different.

CHAPTER FIVE
BLAIR

Sweat coats my body from head to toe, and I kick off my heavy blankets, practically gasping for air.

Shit. I knew the old heater still had a fighting spirit, but I didn't expect it to go so hard. Though I suppose that's my fault for busting it up to the highest setting. My whole body shivered from the time I got out of Oxley's pickup to the minute I curled into bed with the heater on full blast. Not to mention my poor little fingers. I could barely feel them as I tried to load up the fireplace. Which reminds me, I need to ask someone about that. Apparently, lighting a fire isn't as simple as I thought. No matter what I did, the big chunks of wood simply wouldn't catch fire. It's like karma's sick joke for not making a better effort for Nana.

Hell, I grew up here. I should know more about surviving than this. I feel like such an idiot.

Despite having a warm shower last night, I can't help but strip down to my birthday suit and have another. There's nothing worse than the feeling of dried sweat coating your body.

After getting myself dressed and ready for the day, I trudge through to the kitchen and sniff out the coffee, letting out a relieved sigh when I find the coffee pods for the fancy machine I bought Nana a few years ago. She loved this machine. Couldn't get enough of it.

I fire it up, and as it comes to life, I head over to the fridge, but when I yank the door open, my eyes settle on the expired jug of milk.

Shit. I'm going to have to make a trip to the grocery store. And while I'm at it, I should probably invest in some better winter apparel. Nana kept all my heavy coats from my teen years, but they're old and worn out. And as for Nana's old clothes . . . I just can't.

Having to make do without milk in my coffee, I settle at the kitchen counter with a notebook and pen while trying to figure out a game plan.

The house is in worse condition than I thought. Well, that's a bit of an exaggeration. It's livable, but it also doesn't stand a chance when up against the modern homes in the area. This was Nana and Pop's first and only home together. They raised my mom here and then raised me, and as much as I love that, it means the house is severely outdated. Hell, there are still lines on my bedroom door frame to mark my height over the years, which only goes to show that the house hasn't been painted since I was a little girl.

I could try to sell it as-is, but I wouldn't just be doing a disservice to myself, I'd be doing a disservice to Nana and Pop. They deserved the best price for the home they loved so much, even if it means extending my stay just a few extra weeks.

Opening my notebook to a fresh page, I jot down everything I need to do.

- Sort through Nana's possessions (create donate or trash piles)
- Sell/trash old furniture
- Remove old wallpaper
- Fix imperfections in the drywall
- Replace carpet
- Upgrade floorboards
- Bring kitchen into the 21st century
- Freshen up bathroom and laundry
- LEARN HOW TO USE FIREPLACE!!!!!!

My gaze lingers on the list. There's a lot to do and certainly a lot that I have no idea how to do. Either way, it's daunting.

I might have to head down to Hardin's Hardware and see if John is still running the show. He was always helpful . . . when he wanted to be. He was quite fond of Nana, so I'm sure he'll be happy to give me a rundown on how to best tackle this job and maybe even suggest a good starting spot.

By the time I have completely filled three whole pages with lists of things I need to do, I grab the keys to Pop's old truck and shove them deep into the back of my jeans pocket. I need groceries if I'm going to have any hope of surviving this, and in order to do that, I'm going to need to tackle the driveway.

Marching out the back door, I head straight to the old shed, slowly creeping toward it. When I was younger, I had irrational fears that a monster lived in here, and despite being a grown-ass woman and knowing better, I still hesitate, certain I'm about to face imminent death.

The shed door creaks open, and I let out a heavy breath, finding the snow shovel right by the front. With lightning speed, I wrap my hand around the handle and yank it out, letting the shed door slam closed behind me.

I sprint away from the monster's lair, my heart pounding as I bring my knees up high with each step through the mounds of snow. Running in the snow has never been a strong point for me.

When I'm a few feet away from reaching the front yard, I stop running, needing to brace my hands on my damp knees to calm myself. That was way too much to deal with before eight in the morning. Either way, I survived the shed monster. Nana would be so proud.

"Holy shit," I mutter to myself, taking deep, heaving breaths. I might have to keep this shovel outside while I'm here. I can't risk facing that shit every damn morning. I don't know how Pop managed to survive it all those years.

Dragging the shovel behind me in the snow, I make my way around the corner only to stop dead in my tracks. My brows furrow with confusion. "What in the ever-loving hell?"

Why the fuck is the driveway and sidewalk already shoveled?

Moving through the thick snow, I step out onto the small pathway that leads from the front porch down to the driveway and gape at it. There's a soft dusting of snow covering the concrete, so whoever did this must have been here during the night.

My heart starts to pound again, and this time it has absolutely nothing to do with the shed monster.

A lump forms in my throat, and as I quickly slip into a world filled with blissful denial, I notice the dangerous icicles that were once dangling from the roof have also disappeared.

There's only one person who would have done this, which means he knows I'm here. Or I can convince myself that some neighborhood kid shoveled the driveway in the middle of the night out of the kindness of his heart. Yeah, that doesn't even sound a little bit believable.

This was Nick. It had to be. Sarah must have let it slip that I was here. Or Oxley. He seemed to know who Nick was. They might be friends, and it's not as though I specifically asked either of them to keep my arrival on the down-low. I just thought I might have a little more time to prepare myself before having to face him. I suppose I should consider myself lucky that he didn't come knocking on the door, or maybe he did and I was in too deep of a sleep to notice.

Shit.

Am I supposed to text him and say thanks or do I pretend that I have no idea who was responsible for this? Hell, maybe I'm wrong all together and Nana had a secret boy toy who came rolling back into town and decided to do her a solid by shoveling the driveway, not realizing she passed.

Who am I kidding? As much as I love living in this blissful denial, I have to face the facts—Nicholas Stone knows I'm home, and as nice as it was for him to clear the snow, I know him better than he knows himself. This was a message, a warning that I can't hide from him for long. He'll be coming for me, and when he does, he won't hesitate to get the answers I've always feared giving him.

With all this extra time on my hands, I make my way around to the garage and spy Pop's old truck. Nana used to drive it every now and then, so for the most part, it should still be good to run. But having said that, I haven't had a single reason to get behind the wheel of a car in the past six years.

Shit. Do I even remember how to drive? Nick was the one who taught me, but that feels like a lifetime ago. Maybe I need to look up a quick YouTube tutorial, but for some reason, I feel that might not be the best idea.

After opening the old garage door and almost giving myself a hernia trying to lift the heavy fucker, I jump into Pop's truck. Even after all these years, it somehow still smells like him. I jam the key into the ignition, and with nerves of steel, I kick over the engine, hoping like fuck it doesn't spontaneously combust.

The truck rumbles beneath me, and a grin cracks across my face. Then just like Pop used to do, I put the truck into reverse and sling my arm over the back of the passenger seat headrest. After backing out of the garage and locking everything up, I get on my way, carefully maneuvering the familiar streets.

The town center is just like I remembered. A big dog park in the very center with a children's playground to the right. The trees I remember planting during a school community project are as tall as mountains with bushy leaves covered in a thin layer of snow.

The stores line the opposite side of the road with parallel parking that I could never really wrap my head around. Getting into the space was fine, but I always messed up reversing out of it. Thinking about it as an adult, it seems so straightforward. I don't know what I was so worried about. It probably goes hand in hand with the shed monster—irrational thoughts creating irrational fears.

Hardin's Hardware is the first in line and probably the biggest store out of them all, and the only store in town that has its own private parking area, but I suppose if the guys with big trucks were always parking in the street, the traffic out here would be a nightmare. Next to that is the post office, and assuming everything is just as it's always been, it's run by Macey Lockwood—a stickler for the rules and one of the biggest pains in my ass. At least, she used to be. Who knows, maybe she's not so bad anymore. Maybe she found herself a man to scratch that itch and she's chilled right out.

Next up is the best coffee shop in town, and the typical first job for the teenagers in town. I worked there for three summers in a row before they realized I was stealing the cookies while on shift and fired me. But I didn't need the job, I just enjoyed the extra shopping money at the end of the week to add something nice to my closet. Sometimes that something nice was for me, and sometimes . . . that something nice was for Nick.

I drive by the dollar store and Blushing's version of Ikea, filled with cheap furniture. There's a real estate office and then finally the grocery store. As I pull into the space outside the grocery store, I try to remember what stores are on the opposite side of the dog park. I know there was a diner and a bakery, but I'm not entirely sure what else this part of town can offer.

Putting Pop's truck in park, I pull the key out of the ignition and make my way to the sidewalk, and just as I go to step toward the grocery store, my gaze flicks back to the real estate office next door. I should probably check if anyone is in today. After all, it'll be good to get a professional's opinion on the upgrades the property needs. Perhaps someone could come by and give me an idea about where the property would fit in the market.

Striding up to the door, a nervousness settles in the pit of my stomach that I don't quite understand, but as I curl my fingers around the handles and find it locked, the nervousness fades away.

"Oh, thank fuck," I mutter to myself, before shoving my hand into my pocket and pulling out my phone. I take a quick picture of the signage in the front window with the realtor's number and their opening hours, and yet for some reason, I don't think I'll actually use it. Perhaps I'm moving too quickly. Maybe I'm not ready to sell the home I grew up in and part with all of those memories. But what other choice do I have? I might never be ready.

Not wanting to dwell on it, I make my way into the grocery store and grin, finding it just as it was six years ago, and for once, I'm glad that some things never change. As I make my way around the store, collecting things and dropping them into my cart, my phone rings, and I quickly bring it to my ear.

"Hey stranger," I say, a smile playing on my lips.

"You're still alive?" Rena asks. "I was worried when I didn't hear from you last night."

"I'm sorry. Yesterday was exhausting. I went to bed holding my phone with the intention of calling, but I think I passed out before I could even find your number."

"That's what I thought." There's a slight pause, and I can almost hear her convincing herself not to ask the one question that's probably been driving her insane, but I'm not surprised when her self-control falters. "Have you seen him yet? Is he just as delicious as he is in all the pictures? Ah, shit. I bet he's even hotter now that he's gone from the boyish early twenties into a real man."

I groan, rolling my eyes. "No. I haven't seen him, and I'm hoping to keep it that way," I say, reaching for a fresh carton of milk before deciding better on it and grabbing another. After all, if I'm going to spend the next few weeks of my life bringing Nana's home into the twenty-first century, I'm going to need all the coffee my body can handle. "Though my driveway just happened to be freshly shoveled when I got up this morning, and while my new bestie who drove me home from the airport was possibly the coolest guy I've ever met, I doubt I left enough of an impression to warrant him plowing my driveway in the middle of the night."

"New bestie?" Rena gasps. "Do I need to feel threatened or excited about the possibility of this guy plowing you?"

"Uggghhhh. Stop. It's not like that. The only thing Oxley is plowing is his boyfriend, and as for the bestie status, I don't know," I tease. "He's a strong contender. We're already sharing all of our secrets, and tomorrow night, he's braiding my hair."

"You're the worst," she mutters before her tone hitches up. "Oh, shit, Airy-Blairy, I have to go. The new yoga instructor just arrived and he's fucking ripped."

"Oh God. Try not to scare this one away."

Rena laughs. "Who knows? Maybe by the end of the session, I'll be the one giving him a workout."

"I'm hanging up," I tell her, rolling my eyes.

The last thing I hear before the line goes dead is Rena's howling laughter, and all too soon, I come back to reality, walking around Blushing's only grocery store. I finish loading up my cart, getting enough things to keep me going for at least a week or two, and as I step up to the register and start unloading my groceries onto the conveyor belt, I find a familiar face, only she finds mine first.

"Well, if it isn't little Blair Wilder," Bessy, the owner of the store chimes with a beaming smile as she scans the groceries. "I haven't seen you in years. How have you been, darlin'? It's a shame to hear about your poor nana. I could hardly believe it."

Did I mention she's a chatterbox?

"It came as a shock to me too," I say, offering her a small smile, not prepared to be bombarded by my own feelings and rampant emotions today.

Bessy mimics my smile and pauses scanning for just a moment to reach out and lay her hand over mine. "You know the whole town is here if you need anything. We all loved Olivia, and we know what a big job you'd be taking on trying to sort through her estate," she tells me. "We missed you at her funeral."

"I know. I'm sorry. I wish more than anything that I could have made it back. I feel as though I've let her down," I say, a pang of guilt spreading through my chest. "As for her estate, it seems to be a bigger job than I realized. Nana and Pop sure collected a lot of things over the years. I need to go through everything and figure out what's meant for safekeeping, what's for donating, and what needs to be thrown away."

"You've definitely got your work cut out for you. I remember your grandparents being in that house when I was just a little girl." Bessy starts scanning my groceries again and I find myself wishing she'd go a little faster. "So, this means you're staying for Christmas?"

"Looks that way."

Bessy's whole face lights up, and I see the scheming before a word has even come out of her mouth. "Oh, that's marvelous news," she says as the rhythmic beep of the scanned products sounds through the store. "We have our annual Christmas fair coming up, and I need a few young ladies for the Catch A Cowboy event. Wait. You're single, aren't you? You didn't bring a special someone along for the trip?"

Ahhh shit.

Bessy has been in charge of the Christmas fair for as long as I can remember. It's always been a great event with all profits from ticket sales going directly to the soup kitchen to allow them to put on a delicious Christmas lunch for the families in need. The Catch A Cowboy event has always been a crowd favorite where the town's most eligible bachelor is placed in the center of a ring with a bunch of thirsty women hovering around, and when the music starts, they run. First to catch the cowboy gets to go out on a date with said cowboy, and while it sounds fun and all, having a date with a random guy is not why I'm here. But on the other hand, it's not like I need to put much effort into being the one doing the catching. Bessy needs volunteers to make the event work, and I need a little fun in my life. I suppose I can run around a ring for a little while and let someone else catch Blushing's most eligible bachelor.

"No, there's no special someone," I admit.

"Oh, wonderful." Bessy claps her hands together in glee. "I'll put your name down for the event."

"Sounds good." I force a smile across my face, but the truth is, while it sounds as though it could be fun, I actually feel a little nervous. I've never played before. I've always been a spectator because when I lived here in my older teens and early twenties, I was never single.

What could possibly go wrong?

CHAPTER SIX
NICK

It's official. I'm not just a concerned citizen doing something nice for a returning neighbor, I've crept well into stalker territory now. I was on my way to Hardin's Hardware to check on John, and the second I saw her pop's old truck making its way through the town center, I couldn't keep myself from pulling to a stop across from the dog park and watching as she went about her morning.

Like I said—I'm a fucking stalker now.

I suppose it's always a good thing to be adding new skills and attributes to your resume, right? So I can only assume this is healthy for me. Ahh shit. Look at me justifying stalking my ex around town. I've officially hit rock bottom.

One thing's for sure though, I'm fucking pissed.

First rule about driving in the snow is to put chains on the fucking tires, you know, if you value your life, of course. But did she bother to do that? Hell no. I should have just left the icicles hanging from her roof last night. At least if one of those dropped and took her out, it'd be a quick, easy death, but by hitting a patch of black ice and skidding off the road, she could end up trapped in a ditch for days without anyone noticing.

Fuck, who am I kidding? If she went missing for even twenty minutes, I'd have a search party out looking for her.

I was supposed to be at Blushing Inn twenty minutes ago to fix a hole in the drywall after a shelf toppled over, but instead, I'm still hovering behind my red pickup, watching Blair through the window of Bessy's grocery store. And fuck, seeing her last night through a window was one thing, but seeing her auburn brown hair and familiar soft smile in the light of morning is entirely different. I've spent years convincing myself that I didn't miss her, but seeing her now after all this time, I can't lie to myself anymore.

She's so fucking gorgeous. Ox was right.

But what I really want to see is the way her eyes light up like Christmas morning when they come to mine, just like they used to. Though something tells me I'm never going to see that again. The next time her eyes light up like that will be when she's looking at another man, and the thought guts me. Hell, how many times has it happened while she was in New York? How many men have come and gone from her life, warmed her bed, while I've been here pining for someone who's never going to want me?

Fuck. I'm such a fool. I know she's not here for me, but why the fuck can't I walk away?

I watch as Blair makes her way through the grocery store, her phone shoved under her ear as she searches through the array of apples, picking out the best ones. I watch as she finishes her phone call and heads to checkout. She chats animatedly with Bessy, who no doubt is welcoming her back to town, but she's probably scolding her for missing Olivia's funeral too.

She comes out of the grocery store with Bessy on her heels, helping her with the groceries before dumping them into the back of her pop's pickup, not even bothering to secure them. But if she wants her groceries rolling around the bed the whole way home, that's not my business.

She moves toward the driver's door when she pauses and glances down the street, her eyes glued to the coffee shop with longing. I roll my eyes. I suppose some things never change. She's always had a coffee addiction, just like the rest of Blushing.

My phone goes off in my pocket, and I swiftly ignore it. It's the third time Jamie from the Inn has called to check that I'm still coming, and yeah, I feel shitty for being late. I'm notoriously on time. I despise being late. It's simply not me, and the fact that I haven't shown up this morning is probably fucking with her head.

Blair waltzes toward the coffee shop, pausing by the real estate office and glancing over the pictures in the window, making my heart race.

Why the hell is she looking at properties for sale? Is she looking to move back here permanently, looking to buy a place of her own? Or is she simply checking out what's on the market so she can sell her grandparents' estate?

Fuck. Why the hell does this mess with my head so much?

What Blair wants to do with her life is none of my business, and yet I need to know. I don't just want the information, I fucking need it. If she's moving back here, I need to know so that I can prepare myself. I can handle her being in town for a few weeks, but if this is a permanent move . . . fuck. I know she'll be fine, but me? I don't know if I can survive having her this close and not being able to call her mine.

Fucking hell. What is wrong with me? I sound like a little bitch. One minute, I'm shoveling her driveway in the middle of the night and the next, I'm sulking on the side of the street at just the idea of her being near me. I need to get a fucking grip.

Blair carries on down the street, disappearing inside the coffee shop, and the moment she's out of view, my gaze shifts back toward the grocery store. If I can count on anyone to give me town gossip and the information I need, it's Bessy. I won't even need to ask her what's going on, she'll simply volunteer the information.

My mantra that Blair is not my problem simply falls out of my head as I dart across the street, slipping inside the store like I've done a million times before.

Catching Bessy's gaze as I walk in, I give her a small smile. "Hey Bess. How're you doing today?" I ask, striding deeper into the store and beelining straight for the snacks, because let's face it, if I'm taking up stalking, I'm gonna need snacks.

"I'm doing well," Bessy says as I grab a few of each before I make my way back to the register and wait for the show to begin. "You know, you're just the man I've been meaning to see."

Bingo.

"Oh?" I ask, feigning cluelessness. "You need something fixed in the store?"

"No. No," she beams, her eyes sparkling with a million little secrets. "I was hoping to sign you up for the Catch A Cowboy event at the Christmas fair next week."

Huh?

Okay. I fucked that one up. Apparently, she doesn't want to tell me all about the familiar face that came strolling through her store barely five minutes ago. Shit, and here I was thinking that Bessy always had my back.

"I, uhh . . . I don't know, Bess," I say, disappointment flooding through my chest. "I thought we agreed that last year was the last time I'd let you twist my arm. I've done it four years in a row. We don't need to make it five. Besides, I'm sure there's some other sorry loser in town who'd be up for running around a ring with screaming women chasing after him." Not to mention, I'm definitely not feeling up to taking some woman on a date when Blair is back in town. Any other time, and maybe I might have agreed. But this is a firm no this year.

"Oh, that's too bad," she says, taking my snacks and scanning them as her eyes do that weird sparkly thing again, warning me that this isn't as innocent as it seems. "You know, I just had a beautiful young woman in the store who's going to be in town for a little while, and she so kindly offered to sign up. It's for a good cause, you know? But if you're not feeling it this year, I'm sure I can find another eligible bachelor who'd be happy to take the winner out."

"I know what you're doing, Bess," I warn, "and it's not going to work."

Bess shrugs her shoulders and lets out a heavy sigh as she goes about ringing up my snacks. "It's fine. If you don't want to do it, I'm not going to pressure you. Besides, I heard Jarrod Sanderson is back on the market. He might be willing to jump in."

Jarrod fucking Sanderson. The asshole who tried to shove his tongue down Blair's throat during senior prom? Over my dead body will that fucker be taking Blair out. Hell, she'll try and win the damn competition just to spite me. Just because she knows I'll be watching every fucking second of it. Hell, even if Jarrod declines the offer and some other random guy steps in, I don't know how I'd feel about the idea of Blair going out with him.

Fuck. What the hell is wrong with me? She hasn't been mine for six years. Why the hell should I care if she goes out on some forced date with some guy she'll probably never see again? I shouldn't feel this possessive of her. God knows she doesn't feel it for me.

"Damn it, Bess," I groan, running my fingers back through my hair as I clench my jaw. I brace my knuckles against the counter, hanging my head as I take a breath. "Fine. I'll do it."

"That's the spirit," she says, way too fucking chirpy for the raging storm brewing inside of me.

"What do you know?" I question, no longer interested in dancing around the topic. Clearly she's come to the conclusion that I know she's back in town, so I might as well try and get the answers I'm looking for. "How long is she here?"

Bess gives me a pitying smile, knowing this shit isn't easy for me. Hell, the whole fucking town knows how hard I took the breakup. They all saw me fall to pieces and had to watch as I slowly put myself back together.

"Your guess is as good as mine," she says, lowering her tone and placing a soothing hand over my fisted one. "She's hoping to sort out her grandparents' estate, and considering the time of year, I can't imagine she'll be able to get it done before Christmas."

Shit. She's here for Christmas. That's a week and a half away.

"And after Christmas? What's she planning to do with the property? Sell it and take her ass back to New York?"

"Sorry, love. She didn't say," she tells me. "I know seeing her again is going to be hard, but do yourself a favor and go and say hello. You're not going to get the answers you're looking for by following her around town and refusing to talk to her."

"What? I'm not—"

"Deny it all you like, Nicholas, but I saw you standing across the street for twenty minutes, gawking through the window of my store like a hungry stray begging for scraps. And if I can notice it with these old eyes, then I can guarantee that eventually, she will too."

Shit.

"I'm just—" The sound of my phone cuts me off, and I let out a heavy sigh before pulling it out, expecting to see another call from the Inn, wanting to make sure I'm still breathing, but instead, I find Oxley's name flashing across the screen. "Sorry, Bess. I've gotta take this."

I put a twenty dollar bill on the counter, despite it being far too much for the handful of things I've purchased, and after scooping up my bag, I press my phone to my ear. "Everything good?" I ask, giving Bessy a polite nod and silently excusing myself from her store.

"I should be asking you that," Oxley grumbles. "I just had a call from Jamie at the Inn thinking you were dead in a ditch somewhere. She said you never showed up this morning, and considering you sound perfectly fine, I can only assume you're being a fucking stalker. Leave the girl alone, Nick."

Fuck. Why is everyone assuming I'm stalking Blair, apart from the fact that's exactly what I've been doing, but do they really need to think so low of me?

"I'm not stalking anybody," I mutter. "Just had to stop and grab something from the store. I'm on my way to the Inn now."

"Mm-hmm. Whatever helps you sleep at night," he says, clearly not buying my bullshit, but it's not as though I completely lied. Just partially. "You know, I was checkin' up on her this morning and drove past her place. She must have gotten up real fucking early to plow all that snow off her driveway."

"Wouldn't know," I mutter, knowing damn well he can see through that as well.

"Just get your ass to work," Oxley says. "Talk to the girl or don't.

It doesn't mean shit to me. But quit stalking her through town. It won't take long before people start noticing, and I hate to break it to you, man, but you stand out like dogs' balls. There's not a damn inconspicuous thing about you."

Rolling my eyes, I march across the road to where I've parked my truck by the side of the dog park, doing everything in my power not to turn my gaze toward the coffee shop. "I'm hanging up," I warn him.

"Yeah, yeah. Whatever," he throws back at me. "Just don't come sulking to me when you get slapped with a restraining order."

The line goes dead, and I shove my phone back into my pocket as I reach my truck, opening the back door and dumping the small bag of snacks onto the seat. Then because I'm a sucker for punishment, my gaze drifts down the road toward the coffee shop, only to find a pair of wide blue eyes staring back at me.

CHAPTER SEVEN
BLAIR

Ahhhhhhhhh fuck.

My eyes widen like two primed and prepped assholes right before world domination.

Nick stands across the street, his gaze locked firmly on mine as he opens the door of his old red pickup, the same truck we lost ourselves in a million times over. And damn it, he looks fucking phenomenal.

Panic soars through my veins, quickly taking hold of all common sense, and before I have a chance to find any semblance of control, I throw myself forward, swan diving over the counter of Blushing's best coffee house and crumbling to the dirty floor.

"Holy fuck. Holy fuck. Holy fuck."

"What the hell do you think you're doing?" the barista demands, gaping at me as though I've lost my mind. And yeah, considering I'm crouched at his feet with my whipped-cream-topped caramel latte now splattered across the back wall of the store, I think that could be a high possibility.

"Holy fuck. Holy fuck. Holy fuck." My tone hitches up an octave, but I can't seem to stop.

"DUUUUUUDE!" the barista reprimands, shoving his booted foot out to catch me in the ribs, and while it's barely a graze, I'll definitely suggest he broke a rib when I tell the story to Rena later.

My eyes flick up, meeting his irritated gaze. "I, uhhhhh . . . shit. I'm sorry. But is the drop-dead gorgeous hunk of a man who looks like he could snap a woman in half with nothing more than his pinky finger still staring this way?"

"What?"

"Just look," I beg, two seconds away from bursting into an uncontrollable flood of tears. Because talking through wild emotions like an adult is apparently beyond me today. I'll skip all the acceptable reactions and hightail it straight to heaving sobs.

"If I tell you, will you get off the fucking floor?"

"I don't think you want my honest answer," I tell him as a clump of whipped cream falls from the wall and splatters on the ground right in front of my feet. "I might be here for a while. We might as well get acquainted. Who knows? It could be fun."

The barista mutters something under his breath before reluctantly leaning forward over the counter to get the best view of the street. "Are you talking about the tall guy with the red pickup who's looking over here and shaking his head like he's never been so disappointed in his life?"

Shit. I know that look well, and considering everything, it devastates me. He has every right to be disappointed in me. Hell, I'm disappointed in myself. The first time seeing Nick in a little under six years and I swan dive over a counter just to avoid him. I've pictured this moment so many times. I always pictured that I would smile and step into his open arms before planting a kiss on his stubbled cheek, maybe letting it linger just a second too long. He would be happy to see me, both of us sharing our lives over coffee and quickly catching up. But swan diving?

What the fuck is wrong with me?

"Yeah," I say, swallowing hard, my hands uncontrollably shaking. "Is he gone?"

"Clearly if he's busy shaking his head, he's not gone."

"Holy fuck."

"Yep. You said that already," he murmurs, grabbing a dish rag and throwing it at me, the damp cloth landing on my arm. "If you're going to take up residence on the floor, the least you can do is start mopping up your latte."

I grumble a string of insults and hope like fuck this guy isn't going to spit in my latte when I ask him to make me a new one, but nonetheless, I grab the dish rag and start cleaning up my mess.

"So, you new in town?" he asks, getting on with other orders, clearly coming to terms with the fact that the sticky floor has just become my new home for the next . . . I don't even know how long.

"Not exactly," I tell him. "I grew up here. I'm just home for the holiday break and then I'll be heading back to New York."

"Ahhh, so I take it Mr. Disappointment out there is an ex then?"

"Is it that obvious?"

"Writing it across your forehead in Sharpie would have been less obvious," he says, glancing back toward the street, his eyes widening just a fraction. "Oh, shit. He's coming."

"WHAT?" I screech, horror gripping me in a chokehold, my palms instantly growing sweaty.

The barista laughs, his lips quirking into an amused smirk. "Chill out. I'm just screwing with you. He took off."

"Oh, thank fuck." My whole body sags, my head dipping forward between my shoulders as I force myself to take deep calming breaths. I don't know what I was expecting, but that certainly wasn't it. And on the off chance that it wasn't Nick who shoveled my driveway last night, he sure as hell knows I'm back now. On second thought, while he certainly didn't look pleased to see me, he also didn't look shocked.

No, Nick definitely knew I was back in town. The only question is, now that I've made an ass of myself, how the hell are either of us supposed to move forward from here? Do I send a text apologizing for my awkwardness, or do I say nothing and pretend the whole thing never happened?

Fucking hell. I'm twenty-eight years old. I should be able to face an ex with poise. But Nick isn't just the average ex, he's the one I let slip through my fingers, the one who got away, and I've regretted it ever since.

One thing is for sure though, he looked incredible.

At twenty-two, we were still just kids with the whole world ahead of us. There were still a few boyish charms about him as he shifted from being a broody teenager into a man, but now, there's no mistaking it. He's almost twenty-nine now, and damn it, it suits him. He's exactly my type.

Even in the snow, he was wearing nothing but a black shirt that hugged his strong arms, showing off the defined muscles beneath, but I'm not surprised by that. He's always been strong and has never opted for wearing a jacket, even during a blizzard. Though, he always kept one in the back of his truck for me because I never could remember to pack my own. Or maybe I did it on purpose, loving how he would offer me his jacket like a perfect gentleman. It always smelled just like him, but I could never work out why because I never saw him wear it.

His hair was cropped short, just as it's always been, and the soft stubble across his jaw has my fingers itching to explore.

Shit. I can't think like this. It's been six years. I was a high school fling . . . Or maybe a little more than that, but I can guarantee a guy like Nick hasn't been waiting around for me to return.

Instant jealousy fires through the pit of my stomach at the thought of him being with anyone else, and yet I have absolutely no right to feel that way. I was the one who broke his heart, I was the one who took off to New York with all these big plans to become some kind of PR guru. Hell, it's not like I haven't tried dating either. I've made plenty of mistakes when it comes to the men I've allowed into my life, and yet Nick was never one of them.

He was the best thing that ever happened to me, and now I've gone and swan-dived behind a fucking counter. Assuming he decides I'm worth talking to, he'll never let me live it down.

Trying to shake off my humiliation, I finish cleaning up my mess before bringing myself back to my feet, only as I stand and lift my chin, I find a petite woman standing right in front of me, her gaze locked on the menu board above my head. "I'll have a—"

"Oh, no. I'm not—"

"Large pumpkin spice latte. Go heavy on the cinnamon and hold the cream," she continues, not bothering to take a moment to realize I've even said a word. "Actually. Make it extra large and add a blueberry muffin."

"I—"

My gaze shifts to the barista, waiting for him to step in and save my ass once again, but finding him swamped as he gets back to filling orders, I let out a heavy sigh and drop my gaze to the tablet before me.

Damn it. Why do I have to have a guilty conscience?

Looks like I'll be working the morning rush, just like I used to all those years ago. After entering her order and hoping like fuck I haven't screwed it up, I glance up at the girl and plaster on my best customer service grin. "And how will you be paying today?"

Two hours later, I crash through the door of Nana's home and collapse onto the old couch, suddenly remembering why I never liked working there. People are mean, but when they haven't got their coffee or think that their coffee is being made far too slowly, they're monsters.

I close my eyes for just a minute before remembering the groceries in the back of Pop's truck, and as I peel myself off the couch, I remember the milk, my whole reason for heading out this morning. I can guarantee it's spoiled having been out of the fridge for so long. But then, it's not like it's a hot day. It was bloody freezing inside Pop's truck while I was busy in the coffee shop. Perhaps it's fine.

After fetching the groceries and shoving the possibly spoiled milk into the fridge, I grab my laptop and drop down at the kitchen counter. If I'm going to fix up this house and sell it, I need to get my shit together, and hell, what better way to distract myself from the brooding, sexy man-meat who just happens to live in town?

God, he looked so good. If only I could see him up close for a second . . . but without him knowing, of course. I don't think I could handle the embarrassment of him bringing up the whole swan dive thing, and I know he will. He simply won't be able to resist. But then, maybe he could. People change a lot in the span of six years. I'm certainly not the same woman I was when I left, so who am I to make assumptions about the things that he can or cannot resist anymore?

The thought has a pang of sadness pulsing through my chest and I do my best to put it aside as I pull out my phone and bring up the photo of the real estate office's storefront I took this morning. Finding the agent's contact number, I enter it into my contacts before hitting call.

I shove the phone against my ear, but as it rings, a wave of nervousness crashes through me and I put the phone down, putting the call on speakerphone as though that could somehow help. I stand, pacing back and forth through the kitchen as the phone remains on the table.

"Blushing Real Estate," a woman's voice chirps a moment later. "This is Estelle."

I scramble for the phone, scooping it into my hands and staring at it as though it could bite me. "Umm . . . hi. This is Blair Wilder. I stopped by your office earlier but you must have been busy," I say, unsure why I felt the need to tell her that. "I uhhh . . . wanted to talk to you about selling my nana's property down on—"

"Blair Wilder? As in Olivia Wilder's granddaughter?"

"Yes, that's me."

"Ahhh, I know her place well," she chimes. "I was wondering what you would decide to do with the property. I'm so sorry for your loss. Olivia was a very welcomed member of our community. Such a shame she's gone."

I press my lips into a hard line, not really knowing how to open my mouth without turning into a blubbering mess. "She was," is all I manage to get out before swallowing over the lump in my throat and trying to get back on track. "So, the plan is to sell, though it does need a little work. It's very dated compared to what's available on the current market so I was hoping to get your advice on what you think would be best. I mean, I don't exactly have the funds to gut the property and start fresh, but I'm pretty good with a paintbrush."

"When were you hoping to get the property on the market?"

"As soon as possible," I admit. "I have a lot going on back in New York, so the sooner the better."

"No problem at all," she says, sounding all too cheery about the fact we're talking about selling my family home. "I'll put you on the schedule for mid-January and we'll go from there."

"Woah. What do you mean mid-January? I was hoping to get the property listed in the next week or so and be home for Christmas, or at least New Year's."

Estelle laughs. "By all means, dear. Fly home for Christmas and New Year's, enjoy yourself, however, the property won't be on the market. This isn't New York where they work themselves to death. We're in Blushing, and here, we close for the holiday period. Besides, there's really no rush. Property in Blushing isn't in high demand, they're not flying off the shelves like hotcakes. Depending on the upgrades you're able to achieve and the price you'd like to get, I suspect we won't be closing on a sale until at least mid-year."

My eyes bug out of my head. "That long?"

"Yes, dear. However, you don't need to remain in Blushing. You can head back home after your renovations, and I'll be in contact with any updates or potential buyers. Just leave me a key for property inspections and we'll be good to go."

"Oh, that easy?"

"It certainly is. The hard part is signing on the dotted line and having to say goodbye."

"That's what I was afraid of," I mutter.

Estelle goes on to give me all her advice on what updates she thinks would be beneficial for sale, and as my gaze sails over the multiple lists stuck to the fridge, I'm pleased to find that I've got most of them accounted for. Fresh paint. Carpets. New fixtures in the bathroom, laundry, and kitchen. Light fittings. And of course, flooring.

The kitchen cupboards are a little outdated, but I'm not exactly made of money, and replacing the kitchen isn't something that's going to happen, but Estelle suggests that replacing the cupboard doors and giving them modern handles would make a world of difference.

Ending the call with Estelle, I grab my lists off the fridge and manically add her suggestions to them before I forget everything she said, and by the time I'm done, I realize that these renovations aren't going to be as simple as I thought. There's a lot to do, and there's no chance in hell I'll have it all done before Christmas.

I suppose for the first time in six years, I'll be spending Christmas in Blushing.

CHAPTER EIGHT
BLAIR

Rena's face appears on my laptop as I scroll through endless paint colors, all of which are doing nothing but giving me one hell of a headache.

"Ugh. You look like shit," Rena tells me from her bathroom as she works on her makeup.

"I feel like shit."

"Sick? Hormonal? Or just a bad day?"

"A seriously bad day," I tell her. "Turns out, the one and only real estate agent in Blushing will be taking the holidays off, so I won't be able to get the house on the market until at least mid-January."

"Oh shit."

"Yeah."

"I mean, on the bright side, that gives you plenty of time to get all the renovations done and bring your nana's place into the twenty-first century."

I roll my eyes and let out a heavy sigh, letting her see just how unhelpful her comment was. "It also means that I'll be stuck in Blushing for Christmas and New Year's."

"And?" she prompts. "It's not like you had plans anyway. I don't recall a single Christmas in the last five years where you haven't spent the day working."

"Yeah, but—"

"No buts," she says, cutting me off. "Take it as a blessing. Use this time to celebrate and reconnect with old friends. Hmm, I don't know. Perhaps enjoy yourself for once. This might just be the break you need before starting your own business, and instead of writing all those to-do lists, maybe you need to be working on a who-to-do list."

My eyes bulge out of my head. "You're insane," I tell her. "Besides, in case you've forgotten, this is Blushing. There's no one to do around here."

Rena grins wide. "You need a naughty list," she continues, scooping up her laptop off the bathroom vanity and walking into her designer kitchen. She grabs a slip of paper and disappears from the screen before returning a second later, holding up the paper that now reads "The Naughty List" and in big bold letters right below it is one all too familiar name.

Nick Stone.

I shake my head before the words even get a chance to tumble out of my mouth. "Okay, did you accidentally hit your head this morning? Are you feeling alright? Because there's no way in hell I'm about to sleep with Nick."

"Come on," she groans. "You always said Nick was the best sex you ever had, and not to mention, from the slight online stalking I've been doing, he's fine as hell. Besides, what are vacations for? Reconnect with the guy, have a few drinks, and screw him for old times' sake. It doesn't need to mean anything, and it's not like I'm asking you to fall in love with him. Just have fun. Have wild, kinky, sweaty sex, and then come home in the new year ready to kill it with this new business."

"You are literally insane. You know that, right?"

"Prude."

"I am not."

"PRUDE!" she says louder before whipping around and shoving "The Naughty List" against her stainless-steel fridge, using every single magnet she owns to keep it in place. She grabs a pen, and just to be an ass, she draws a little box right next to Nick's name, just waiting to be checked off. "There. That looks better."

"You need to take that down."

Rena looks back over her shoulder, grinning at me through her screen. "And remove a to-do list before all the tasks on said list have been completed?" she gasps, mimicking the bullshit I've spouted at her over the years. "I would never."

"You're such an asshole."

Rena laughs. "An asshole? I'm just doing my duty as your best friend and looking out for you and your sad little underused coochy.

Now, if I really wanted to be an asshole, I'd take a photo of your new naughty list and accidentally send it to Nick on all of his socials, and if he just happened to miss that, then don't be surprised if you happen to see a plane flying across Blushing with a banner hanging from the bottom saying Hey Blair, don't forget to fuck Nick."

"You're seriously messed up. You know that, right?"

"I'm just trying to look out for you, Airy-Blairy. Though, come to think of it, I don't think you have anything to worry about. From the looks of it, Nick doesn't use his socials. None of them look like they've even been touched in years."

A grin pulls at the corner of my lips. "That's Nick for you," I tell her. "He's always hated social media. I made those accounts for him before I left for college, but I don't think he ever really used them apart from the occasional post here and there. He's more of the here-and-now type. He doesn't like living through a screen."

"Makes sense," she says. "Have you had a chance to say hi yet?" I scrunch my face, and she instantly picks up on my hesitation. "What did you do?" Rena questions, her tone shifting with a deep suspicion.

"I uhhh . . . almost ran into him this morning."

"Almost? What's that supposed to mean?"

"I was in the coffee house, and as I looked out the window, he was just kinda there staring back at me."

Rena leans in closer to the screen, her gaze narrowing on mine. "And?" she prompts.

"And it wasn't my finest moment. I panicked," I tell her, feeling that same anxiety I felt this morning creeping up over me. "I dove over the counter and hid. It was humiliating."

"Oh shit," Rena booms. "I would have paid to see that."

"You have no idea just how glad I am that you weren't here to see it," I mutter. "But I feel like shit. The dude behind the counter said he shook his head and looked disappointed and it just . . . I don't know. It made me feel terrible. After all these years and the hurt I caused him, I didn't even have the courage to smile and wave or say thank you for plowing my driveway. I wasn't . . . ready."

Rena offers me a sad smile, and because she's been my best friend for so long, I know she's about to give me the kind of advice that's going to hit me right in the feels. "Girl, he was your first love, and despite how you say you've moved on and built your life here in New York, you'll always be ridiculously in love with him. I see it in your eyes every time his name comes up. He's the one who got away, and now that you're back home, you have a chance to make things right."

"I'm not in love with him," I say in a small voice, knowing damn well I'm lying.

Rena scoffs. "Really? You're going to hit me with that shit?"

Letting out a sigh, I drop my gaze, unable to meet her stare. "I'm scared, Rena."

"I know you are," she tells me. "But what are you actually scared of? Facing the hurt you caused him and dealing with the guilt that comes along with that, or are you scared that he doesn't love you anymore?"

Tears well in my eyes, and I hastily wipe them away, hating how effortlessly she can make me face my own demons. "I don't know," I tell her honestly. "I'm scared of it all. I don't know what I'm supposed to do or what to even say. How am I supposed to just walk up to a man I hurt like that?"

"That's for you to figure out, Blair. I can't help you with that, but what I do know is that the longer you put it off, the harder it will get."

"You know, I really don't like it when you force me to deal with my emotions."

"I know, and given any other circumstances, I would have let it go, but you're back home, in the town where you first fell in love with Nick, and I can't help but feel that this is some kind of Christmas gift. I'd hate for you to waste it. Besides, if you don't at least try, you and I both know that when you get back to New York, you'll regret it. You need to know where you stand and if there's a chance that you can find your happiness again."

My head falls into my hands as I brace my elbows on the table. "And if he's moved on and doesn't love me anymore?"

"You get really fucking drunk."

Shit.

Rena and I talk for another hour, going over all of my ideas for my branding for the new business before it somehow shifts into paint colors for Nana's home, and by the time she has to end the call, I'm all talked out.

It's already been such a huge day and is well after three in the afternoon, but as I look around the home I grew up in, I realize Rena was onto something. This is my chance to relax before starting my new business. I'm back in my hometown where I once thought of

Christmas as the most magical time of year. Perhaps it's time for me to try and find that magic again.

But how? Nana was always the brain behind our Christmas traditions. She decorated our home and blasted Christmas carols through the house from the 1st of December. She had a roaring fire going every day, and the warmth inside the house was like none other.

How the hell am I supposed to replicate that without her?

Digging out all the Christmas decorations won't be hard, but I don't even have a tree. Pop used to take us every year to pick out the best one, but without him, how the hell am I supposed to chop one down? Hell, how am I supposed to get it in the back of his truck, let alone carry it into the house?

Shit. Maybe I'm insane for thinking I can do this.

I'm just about ready to give up when I spy the photograph of Nana and me from my college graduation stuck to the fridge, and I know without a doubt that she would be so disappointed in me for even considering giving up. I can just hear her telling me, *You're a Wilder, Blair, and Wilders do not give up.*

Fuck it. I'll wing it. It's up to me to make the magic now.

Glancing at the clock, I realize I have just enough time to get out to the old Christmas tree farm and ponder over what little selection they have left, chop down the biggest one I can find, haul its piney ass into the back of Pop's truck, and have just enough time to stop by Hardin's Hardware on the way home and pick up some spackle and a few paint samples.

With a newfound determination pounding through my veins, I

grab my wallet, keys, and phone off the counter and head straight out the door. It's not until I'm halfway to the Christmas tree farm that I realize my coat is still hanging over the coat rack by the front door.

Fuck. This is going to suck. But it's not like I need to be there for hours. I'll be quick. I just need to get in, pick a tree, and get straight back in the truck. How long could it possibly take?

The Christmas tree farm is on the outskirts of town, nearly a good forty-minute drive. In the summer, this drive is absolutely spectacular with the expansive views of the trees and rolling hills in the distance, but in the dead of winter, it's nothing but a white blob. It's an overcast day with a steady flow of snowfall, but it's nothing I can't handle. As long as it's not storming, I'll consider myself lucky.

A soft smile settles over my face as I reach the main entrance of Old McDonald's Farm, and I slow down before pulling into the parking lot. There are a few cars around, but from the looks of it, it's clear that the majority of Blushing has already come and gone, probably leaving nothing but the scraps behind.

My determination keeps me going. I'm going to save what's left of this Christmas and somehow make it magical, even if it means scouring every last inch of this farm for the best tree on the lot.

I drive right up to the top of the farm, finding the best parking space. My gaze lingers on the surrounding trees as I pull into the space, trying to figure out the best place to start my search, and just as my foot lifts off the gas and shifts toward the brake, my tires hit a patch of black ice and I lose control.

Fear pounds through my veins as Pop's truck slides toward the ditch in front of the parking spaces, and I slam my foot onto the brake as a raw scream tears from the back of my throat. "OH FUCK," I panic, desperately trying to gain control, but it's no use, there's too much momentum.

The truck launches forward, the front end dropping heavily into the ditch and coming to a crunching stop as my heart thunders wildly in my chest. "Holy fucking shit," I mutter, my eyes wide as I white knuckle the steering wheel.

I take a moment, barely able to believe that just happened, all too aware that if Pop were here he would be cursing me out right about now.

A sharp knock sounds at the window, and I whip my head around, finding a familiar face staring back at me. "Miss," Billy McDonald from my high school calls out, his hands braced against the glass to see past the fog glued to the window. "Miss, are you alright?"

He tries the handle, and the door pops open just enough that I'll be able to squeeze through. "Miss," he says again, his voice filled with the kind of calmness that has me finally catching my breath. "Are you okay? Are you hurt?"

My brows furrow as I take him in, standing in knee-deep snow. "I, ummm . . . yeah. I think I'm okay," I say, embarrassment gripping me in a chokehold.

"Can you get out?"

Cutting the engine, I grab my things and unbuckle my seatbelt before wriggling over to the edge. There's a fallen tree in the bottom of the ditch keeping the door from opening any wider, and Billy heaves it back, giving me just a little more space.

He offers me his hand, and I gingerly take it as I drop out of the truck, my feet instantly sinking into the deep snow. "Thanks," I say with an awkward smile as he points out the best place for me to brace my foot to help me up. There's an older gentleman standing just at the top of the ditch, right where Pop's truck was supposed to be parked. He reaches down and grips my arm to help pull me the rest of the way out of the ditch.

He's also familiar, and I can't help but wonder if this is Billy's father, the original Old McDonald. "I, uhhh . . . I'm really sorry," I say to him as Billy climbs out of the ditch, using the back of Pop's truck for leverage. "I'm not the best driver, but I swear, if I knew I'd end up in a ditch, I would have picked a different space."

The old man grins, his gaze shifting over the truck before looking at the road like some kind of investigator. "You should really have chains on your truck," he says in an accusatory tone.

His son moves in beside me, offering me a polite smile before glaring at his father. "Knock it off, Pops. It's not her fault. She hit black ice," he says before shifting his gaze back to mine. "But he's right. You really should have chains on your tires. You were lucky today, but if you were on the highway, it could have been fatal."

My face scrunches. "I know, I've been meaning to do it, but I haven't had a minute to figure it out. I only just got back into town."

"Ahh, you're . . . wait. Why does your face seem so familiar to me?"

"Blair Wilder," I say, really starting to notice the chill in the air as the adrenaline begins to wear off. "We were in high school together.

Pretty sure you sat behind me during History all through senior year."

Recognition flashes in his bright blue eyes. "Ahhhh yeah. That's right. You're Nick's girl."

"Yeah, something like that," I say, not willing to get into it as his father shuffles over, getting a good look at Pop's truck in the ditch, probably trying to figure out where the hell to go from here. "What's the diagnosis? Is the truck a lost cause?"

"Nah, nothing a good tow can't handle," the old man says, patting the back of the truck like he was spanking a woman's ass. "We'll get her back on her feet. Might not happen today though. Do you have someone you can call?"

Shit.

My mind goes straight to Nick, but there's no way in hell I can call him for a ride, not after I dove behind the coffee house counter this morning. My ego is far too bruised to have to face that one today. I suppose I could call Oxley, but his number is still on that little slip of paper on my kitchen counter.

Just fucking great.

I give Billy and his father a forced smile. "Yeah, I'll figure out a way home," I tell them, wondering how Sarah would feel about giving me Oxley's number. "In the meantime, are there any good trees left?"

"Sure thing," Billy's father says, waving a hand toward the main entrance of the farm as I really start to shiver, cursing myself for not remembering my damn coat. "Follow me, darlin'."

CHAPTER NINE
NICK

The drywall at the Inn looks fucking perfect as I stand back, surveying my work for the day. I'll have to come back tomorrow to sand it and put a coat of paint over it, but for now—fucking perfect. I pride myself on offering a high standard to my customers, and so far, there hasn't been a job that I haven't been able to ace.

I pack up my tools, walking in and out of the Inn as I load my truck with all of my shit. I'm just about done when my phone rings, and for just a moment, I consider letting it go to voicemail. After the shitty morning I had when Blair dove over the coffee house counter just to avoid me, I really can't be fucked to deal with someone else's emergency.

Seeing Billy McDonald's name flash across my screen, my brows furrow. I was never close with Billy in high school and never had anything to do with him after it either. We've run into each other occasionally at the local Bar & Grill and had a drink together, but as far as friendship goes, that's about it. Billy considers himself a bit of a handyman, so he's never needed my help or input, so the fact he's calling now is more than suspicious.

After accepting the call, I lift my phone to my ear, hoping like fuck he doesn't have an emergency that will keep me from going straight home to crash. "Hey, Billy. What's up?"

"Hey man. Look, I ummm . . . I know it's none of my business and that your girl said she could figure something out, but she's been walking up and down the farm for twenty minutes and hasn't even looked at a damn tree. And considering the way she's talking to herself, I'm pretty sure she's having a psychotic break."

My brows furrow, and I pause on the bottom step of the porch that leads to the grand entrance of Blushing's one and only inn. "What the fuck are you talking about?"

"Oh . . . you don't know?" he questions. "She said she'd call someone to help. I just figured she was talking about you."

"The fuck is going on, Billy?"

"Blair," he states. "She's down at the farm. She hit a patch of black ice and her truck is buried in a ditch. She really should have chains on her tires, man."

My eyes widen, my heart racing as I launch myself toward my truck, desperate to get to her. "Is she alright?" I rush out. "Is she hurt?"

"Nah, she's fine. Maybe a little shaken, but she seemed more interested in picking a fucking tree. I mean, shit. This girl's priorities are out of whack," he laughs to himself. "As for your girl's truck, I don't know what you wanna do with it. I don't think it's damaged, but there's no telling until we get it out of the ditch. You'll probably need to call a tow."

Fucking hell. This bastard seems to be putting a lot of responsibility for Blair's truck on me. "She's not my girl."

"Wait. What?" Billy says. "You're not together? I figured you two were doing the whole long-distance thing. But she's single? Fuck. Why didn't you start with that? Listen, don't worry about coming out here. I'll get it sorted out for her."

Over my dead fucking body.

"You even look at her wrong, and I'll gut you like a fucking fish," I warn him, still remembering the aggressive way he tried to pick up girls in high school. "I'll be there in twenty."

Throwing myself into the cab of my truck, I take off, not sparing a moment to even bother telling the staff at the Inn that I will be back tomorrow. All I can seem to do is imagine Blair running off the road over and over again inside my head, and the more it plays on repeat, the faster I drive.

It's usually a good forty-minute drive from the town center, but from the Inn, I should be able to get there in twenty minutes, twenty-five at most, though I'm certainly creeping well over the speed limit.

The whole drive, my mind whirls with the worst-case scenario, and despite Billy telling me that she's absolutely fine, I can't possibly believe it until I've seen her with my own eyes. Hell, what the fuck is she even doing trying to get a Christmas tree?

I get halfway to the farm when my phone blares to life, and I find Oxley's name flashing on the screen. "What's up?" I say, not in the mood for pleasantries.

"I just got a call from Blair. Apparently, she had some kind of accident and ended up in a ditch—"

"Yeah, I—"

"I won't be coming past there for another few hours," he continues, not bothering to hear what I have to say. "She sounded desperate, man. I know you're having a hard time with her being back and all, but I think you're gonna have to head out and help her."

I let out a heavy sigh, gripping the steering wheel just a little too tight as jealousy tears through me like the blade of a rusted knife. She called him. Not me. "I'm already on my way," I say, just as I reach the portion of the highway that gets shitty cell service. "I gotta go, but I'm taking care of it."

"Thank fuck," he says, his voice crackling through the poor connection. "Let me know if you need a hand with the truck."

I end the call, not bothering with a goodbye as the crackling gets worse, and within the space of thirty seconds, I lose service altogether. It's not until I pull into the parking lot of Old McDonald's Farm that my service returns, but I couldn't care less as I see the tail end of her truck sticking up out of a ditch, not a fucking tire chain in sight.

"Fuck me," I mutter, pulling to a stop across the lot, already trying to figure out a game plan. I should have figured out a way to put those damn chains on her tires, then none of this would have happened.

So much for my mantra—she's not my problem.

I should have known I was full of shit the second I started telling myself that. In reality, whether Blair considers herself mine or not, to me, she'll always belong right by my side.

Getting out of my truck, I lean up against the hood as I scan the farm, looking for the woman who's been the center of my whole fucking world since I was sixteen years old. I find her only a moment later and fury instantly ripples through me.

She's not wearing a damn coat. What kind of self-respecting adult goes out in the middle of winter without a fucking coat? Blair fucking Wilder, that's who.

I arch a brow, watching as she drags the biggest fucking tree she could possibly find through the snow, heaving it inch by inch. I have to admit, I would have loved to stand back and watch as she cut that bastard down. That would have been the best entertainment Blushing could ever offer, but I'll have to settle with just the thought of it.

Blair pauses a moment, dropping the base of the tree and stretching out her back as she takes a second to catch her breath before bending back down and picking it up again. Bits of the tree are left behind as she drags it through the snow, and as she inches it closer and closer to the back of her pop's truck, it occurs to me that she thinks she's somehow getting that truck out of the ditch.

Is she in-fucking-sane? Does she think she'll just drop back down into the ditch, wade through the knee-high snow, wrestle her way inside the cab, and reverse it out of there?

Fuck me.

I shift on my feet, crossing my arms over my chest as I watch her, and within the blink of an eye, her whole body stiffens, realizing she's not alone. And judging by the way she doesn't immediately snap back into action, she knows damn well it's me.

Blair huffs and puffs as she gets back to work, dragging the tree just a little bit faster, but the deeper into the snow she gets, the harder it becomes, and it's clear from the strain in her eyes that she's more than struggling.

"What's wrong? No counters to throw yourself behind this time?" I ask, slowly striding toward her, almost terrified of getting too close. But damn it, I need to be close, need to feel the warmth of her skin against mine, need to breathe in that sweet scent. "We can go inside and you can dive behind Billy's counter if it'll help."

Out of all the things I could have said to her, that's the fresh bullshit I chose to go with? Just fucking great. Though, I never claimed to have my shit together, especially when it comes to Blair Wilder.

"What do you want, Nick?" she throws over her shoulder. "I'm busy, and I sure as hell don't need your help."

Okay. So apparently neither of us is capable of being mature adults about this. Fine by me.

I let out a frustrated scoff and continue toward her, not sure what the fuck I'm feeling. Anger pulses through my veins at the same time that adoration and pure want overwhelm my system. I need to be close to her, if only for a second.

Making my way across the lot, I move in beside her, and she tenses, releasing her hold on the tree as she whips around to fix me with a heavy stare, only I ignore it as I dive for the stupid tree. "What the hell do you think you're doing?" Blair seethes as I haul the fucker over my shoulder and make my way back toward my truck. "Hey. I'm talking to you."

I scoff again, rolling my eyes simply because I know how much it gets under her skin. I don't respond as I reach my truck and settle the tree into the back as Blair finally finds the courage to storm after me. "I don't need your help," she spits, crossing her arms over her chest, unaware of the way the movement pushes her full tits together.

"Right. Because you had it under control," I tell her, arching a brow and trying my hardest to hold on to what little control I have left. "What was your big plan, Blair? I don't see Billy or his old man around. How were you planning on getting that tree in the back of your truck, huh? How were you planning on getting your spoiled ass home?"

Blair clenches her jaw, fury rippling through her stare. "I would have figured it out."

I shake my head, turning back to my truck and throwing a strap over the tree to secure it. "Before or after you froze to death?"

"God. You're such an asshole."

"Me? I'm the asshole?" I ask, whipping back around, more than ready to tear her to shreds.

"Yeah, you are. I don't know if you've noticed, but I'm not some damsel who needs saving, especially from you. I can take care of myself. I don't need you constantly showing up and trying to do things for me."

"Oh, my bad. Tell me, how did you like shoveling your fucking driveway this morning?"

"Shit. I'd almost forgotten about that God complex of yours," she throws back at me. "I was more than ready to shovel the driveway. It's not my problem that you chose to put your big-ass nose into my business and do it before I could even get a chance. Tell me, what time did you come by? Was it early this morning? Or was your desperation clawing at you so much that you couldn't possibly wait that long? Were you creeping through the streets in the middle of the night while the neighbors slept?"

I turn back around, getting busy with the straps, but apparently she hasn't had enough. "What are you looking for? A thank you?" she scoffs. "Because in case you didn't notice, I didn't ask you to do that."

"That's right, because little miss independent Blair Wilder doesn't ask for shit. Believe me, I'm more than aware," I tell her, hating that pang of ugliness inside of me that's lingered for six long years since the day she refused to ask if I'd even want to come to New York with her. "But when did your normal human decency and morals fade away? Was it the second you got to New York or did it slowly chip away over the years? Because I sure as fuck know that your grandparents didn't raise you like that. Around here, when someone does something nice for you, whether you asked them to or not, you say thank you."

Fuck. Why do I have to love her like this?

Blair seethes at me, her gaze narrowed into lethal slits, and I can almost feel her laser stare tearing into me. She doesn't respond, refusing to say thank you out of principle. But I know her better than anyone on this goddamn planet. I know everything about her, know the way she sounds when she sleeps, know the way she tastes. And because I know her so well, I know just how grateful she is that she didn't have to plow her fucking driveway. Don't get me wrong, Blair doesn't mind a bit of physical labor, but if she can avoid it, she will.

Keeping my hands moving on the straps, I meet her furious stare. "Get in the truck."

"Like hell I'm getting in your truck."

I clench my jaw, resisting the urge to tighten the strap so much that the tree snaps in half. "Get in the fucking truck, Blair. I'm not asking again."

She scoffs, turning away and striding toward her pop's pickup. "Thanks for the offer," she spits over her shoulder, emphasizing the word thanks like it's poison on her tongue. "But you've lost your mind if you think I'm about to go anywhere with you."

Don't do it. Don't fucking do it.

Shit.

I storm around the back of my truck, my strides eating up the distance between us with ease, and before I know it, my hands are on her toned waist, hauling her over my damn shoulder. Blair squeals as I turn around and make my way back to my truck, every step accompanied by a firm beating against my back. But damn, all I can think about is the way she smells like every fucking dream I've had since the day I first met her in high school.

"I swear to God, Nick. If you don't put me down—"

"You'll what?" I demand, tearing open the passenger side door and depositing her into the seat. "You'll have a tantrum and run away to New York so you can avoid having to deal with anything real?"

She glares at me, and I take a step back, closing the door between us before I end up with those full lips crushed against mine, because God knows if I touch her like that, if I even think about her like that right now, I won't be able to stop until we're both lying in the back of this damn truck, covered in sweat with her throat raw from screaming my name.

With the tree properly secured, I get into my truck, overwhelmed by her scent in the air. "Where's your coat?" I ask, kicking over the old engine and easing onto the gas as I turn the truck around, more than ready to get out of this old farm and back to reality.

"I'm fine," she mutters.

"You're blue."

She rolls her eyes, and I can't help but reach into the backseat of the truck and grab my coat before tossing it at her, because let's face it, neither of us is capable of being mature about this right now. I don't say a word and neither does she as she shoves her petite arms into my coat, and I don't miss the way she pulls it tight around her, sinking her face into the soft material just like she used to, but back then, it was because she was breathing in my scent on the coat . . . now, I'm not quite so sure.

Turning out of the farm's parking lot, I hit the highway and sail back toward Blushing.

With every silent passing second, the tension rises in the truck, and

I'm forced to put my window down just so I can take a deep breath without feeling as though I'm dying inside.

Blair stares out the window, her fidgeting hands picking at her deep red nail polish. It's the only tell that she's just as messed up as I am right now.

The silence is torture, and the longer I sit here beside her, unable to call her mine, the harder it gets. My fingers tighten on the steering wheel, my knuckles turning white until I can't take it a second longer. "You just left, Blair. You didn't even give me a chance to fight for us."

Silence. Fucking silence.

"Nick, I—"

"No," I say, cutting her off as I shake my head. "I don't want your bullshit excuses for how you could so easily throw it away without a fucking care in the world."

"Is that really what you think? That I just got up one day and walked out the door without even considering what it meant for the people around me? Do you honestly think that little of me?"

"You know I don't, Blair. I've always loved you more than life itself, but that's exactly what you did. I barely got a conversation. You were here one day, and we were planning to build a fucking life together, and then the next day you were gone."

Tears well in her eyes but she focuses her attention out the window, concealing her face as she discreetly wipes her tears onto my coat. "I know you, Nick, better than anyone," she says, her voice breaking with the most intense heartache that kills something inside of me. "You never would have come to New York with me. You love it here in

Blushing. This is your home, but I needed to see what was out there for me, even if it meant tearing myself in two. You never would have come with me."

I gape at her, my heart thundering out of control. "Of course I fucking would have," I throw at her, watching as her wide gaze whips back toward mine, staring at me in horror, as if only now just realizing how deeply she fucked up. "I would have followed you to the fucking ends of the world, but you didn't even give me the fucking option. You walked away without a fucking care in the world, and you didn't give a shit what you were leaving behind. You didn't even ask me, Blair. You didn't give me or us a fucking chance."

Her tears fall faster, and she presses her trembling lips together. I focus my attention back on the road, unable to handle the hurt in her eyes. "Was it even real to you?" I ask softly, fearing her response. "I thought we were starting a life together."

"How could you even ask me that?" she asks, her voice wavering. "Every second of it was real for me. You have no idea how much I've hurt over these past six years, how much it aches just to think about you moving on."

She pauses for just a second as if searching for the words she's been wanting to say, the ones that have been buried deep inside of her for six long years. "Walking away from you was the biggest mistake of my life, and I regret it every fucking day," she tells me, her voice barely a whisper between us. "I had goals that were so much bigger than Blushing, and I hate that I hurt you, but I was never going to be content until I'd achieved the things I needed to achieve. I'm sorry,

Nick. I'm so fucking sorry. You have no idea what leaving you did to me, but do you honestly think I'd make a decision like that lightly? Why the hell do you think I haven't been able to come home in six years? I haven't been able to breathe without you, let alone come back here and face the hurt I put you through."

"Blair—"

"Please just . . . don't," she says. "That's not fair. Coming at me like that and saying that you would have followed me to New York. You don't think I considered that? You don't think I knew that you would have followed me anywhere I went? Of course I knew, but you would have been miserable. You would have hated it, and I would never have put you through that. What kind of selfish asshole would that have made me? I didn't want you to sacrifice your happiness for my own."

"But walking away from me . . . that's exactly what you did."

"I know," she whispers, hanging her head, her hands balling into fists in her lap as if resisting the urge to reach out to me. "Either way it played out, we both would have lost."

"You didn't lose, Blair. You got your big shiny career in New York. You got exactly what you wanted."

She scoffs. "If only that were true."

CHAPTER TEN
BLAIR

Memories of the times I've spent with Nick in this truck take me by storm, and every single one of them destroys me. This really isn't how I envisioned my day going. It's one thing after another with Nick, but one thing is for sure, he's still the most infuriating man I've ever met.

The swan dive behind the coffee house counter was an unfortunate incident, but it left us both in our feels and unable to have a real conversation. Hell, we're both screaming at each other, saying everything we've been needing to say, and yet neither of us truly hears what the other is trying to convey.

Like I said—infuriating.

There's something about Nick that brings out the inner demon inside of me, and yet, he can also bring out the best parts of me too, parts I'm sure are now dead and gone.

The cab falls into silence again, and as Nick flies down the highway, lost in his thoughts, we approach the local cemetery. My back stiffens as I look in, knowing that both Nana and Pop are in there, and yet out of all of the headstones, I have no idea which ones belong to them.

Undeniable grief and guilt catch me off guard, and my eyes fill with tears as a heaviness weighs down on me. A lump forms in my throat, and I struggle to breathe over it, barely able to catch my breath.

What kind of granddaughter doesn't know where her grandparents' resting place is?

Fuck. What does that make me? Am I really that so caught up in my own fear of facing this very man beside me that I failed to be the granddaughter they deserved? I couldn't even find the courage to come home for Nana's funeral. And when Pop died? Fuck . . .

Nana told me not to come, that I needed to focus on my work in New York and that she was alright, but at the end of the day, whether she had undeniable strength or not, I didn't come home when she needed me most.

My heavy sobs rip through the silence, and I drop my face into my hands, unable to handle the overwhelming guilt tearing through me. "Fuck," Nick says with alarm, his gaze shooting between me and the road as he hurries to pull over right by the damn cemetery. "Baby, are you okay? I didn't mean to go at you like that. I'm sorry. I couldn't—"

"It's not you," I choke out over the lump in my throat. "I deserved that and so much more."

"Then what . . ." His words trail off as if only now realizing where we are, and as he gazes out to the cemetery, a heaviness floods through his mesmerizing blue eyes. "Shit. I didn't think . . . I should have gone the long way around."

I shake my head, not wanting him to bear the weight of this. It's on me, all of it. I'm the one who didn't come home, I'm the one who hasn't dealt with the grief of losing Nana, and I'm the one who failed to be present enough to even know where either of my grandparents are buried.

"Do . . . Do you want to go in?" he asks, his hand reaching out and hesitantly taking mine, his thumb gently brushing over my knuckles and drawing my whole attention.

My hand shifts under his, my heart thundering as I turn my palm just enough to hold onto his, desperately needing the comfort. "I . . ." I pause, shaking my head before glancing back toward the cemetery. "I don't . . . I'm not sure I'm ready."

The tears continue and Nick breaks, reaching for me and hauling me across the cab until I'm straddled over his lap. His strong, warm arms close around my waist and hold me against his chest. As instinct kicks in, I fold myself into him, burying my face in the curve of his neck, right where I've always belonged.

The grief tears through me, and he holds me tight, refusing to let go as his hand gently roams up and down my back. It's like coming home, and despite the grief and chill of winter roaring around us, I've never felt so warm.

I cry and cry. Letting out the grief and torment I've felt over the past six years, hating myself for the pain I've put everyone through for my own selfish desires. Hating how I abandoned Nana and Pop, hating how I left my friends behind, hating how I've failed my own heart.

I grieve for the life I could have built with Nick, knowing the dream we always shared died the day I turned my back and walked away, the day I tore him to shreds. Yet here he is, offering me comfort in one of my darkest moments.

Nick dips his head, his forehead resting against my shoulder, and as his lips gently brush across the base of my neck, I suck in a breath.

God. What I wouldn't give to feel those lips on mine.

Seconds turn into minutes when I finally pull myself together and sit back on his lap, wiping the last of my tears off my cheeks. "Sorry," I say, barely able to look at him. The very last time I saw him, this is exactly how we were sitting, in this very truck, only it was his heart that was breaking, not mine. "I didn't mean to fall apart like that."

Nick reaches out, his fingers brushing beneath my chin and raising it just enough to meet my eyes. "You know I'm always here," he tells me, his hand hesitantly falling to my thigh. "No matter what's going on between you and me, or how many fucking miles are between us. If you're hurting, I've got you."

I swallow hard, and not knowing how to respond, I scramble off his lap, unable to handle the intensity in his eyes. "I, ummm . . . thanks," I say, my gaze dropping to my hands in my lap, the loss of his warmth hitting me like a freight train and leaving me gasping for air.

Words fail me, and instead of trying to figure something out, I simply nod toward the steering wheel. "I'm good if you want to keep going," I tell him. "I'll come back another time . . . when I'm ready."

"You know, she's not going to hold it against you," he tells me, reaching for the stick shift. "She might haunt your ass for a while, but she'll understand that it's too hard."

I scoff, picturing it so clearly, and as the truck idles, ready to get back on the road, Nick meets my stare. "You know, just because you're not ready to walk in there and physically stand in front of a piece of stone that says her name, doesn't mean that you're not ready to acknowledge her. You're living in the home where you made all of those memories. You're with her every time you crash onto that old sofa or when you drive around Blushing. Her essence is within you, it's inside this town and her home. Her resting spot means nothing. It's just a plot of dirt."

"You sound as though you're talking from experience," I say, knowing damn well he hasn't lost a single person in his life.

Something hardens in his eyes, and he turns his attention back out the windshield. "I'm not the same person you used to know," he mutters, each of his words filled with a heaviness I can't quite understand. And with that, he goes to hit the gas, only the truck rumbles before the engine cuts out, taking the heating right along with it.

"The fuck?" Nick mutters, reaching for the key and twisting it in the ignition again, only for the old truck to swiftly die again.

Horror blasts through my chest, my eyes widening with the realization that we're trapped on the side of the road, right outside a damn cemetery. "Nick," I gasp, my heart thundering for a whole new reason.

"It's fine," he says, trying to kick it over again, getting exactly the same result.

"NICK!"

"What?" he says, shrugging it off. "She's an old truck. What do you expect me to do? I've been meaning to get her serviced for months."

Panic soars through my chest. "This is so not happening."

Nick scoffs, reclining his seat and making himself comfortable. "You better fucking believe it's happening," he says, bracing a deliciously muscled arm behind his head and flashing me the most panty-melting smirk I've ever seen. "Get comfortable, B. There's no cell service out here. And unless someone just happens to drive by and rescue our asses, we're stuck until someone back home notices we're gone. Unless you fancy a walk, of course? But it'll be a long one, and I can't guarantee that you'll make it home before the frostbite sets in."

Fuck.

This day just keeps getting better.

CHAPTER ELEVEN
NICK

Okay, so I may be acting chill about this whole situation, but inside, I'm fucking panicking. It's not the prospect of freezing to death on the side of the road that scares me, it's the fact that I'm stuck in a confined space with Blair Wilder, and my only option of escape is to dig myself a grave right next to my mother's and fall straight into it.

For some reason, the whole walking back to Blushing option doesn't seem very appealing. Don't get me wrong, I love a good workout, love it even more when it has everything to do with two bodies getting sweaty together, but walking through the snow on the side of an icy road, getting cold, numb feet just isn't for me. I'd rather grill Blair and figure out when the hell she expects to get her ass back to New York so we can both move past the agony of having to face each other once again.

"Why the hell didn't you keep up with your servicing?" Blair demands, looking at me as though I planned this. I mean, sure, it isn't ideal, but being forced into a confined space might just be what we need.

"Have you seen the truck? It's a million years old. If I take it into the shop, I'll come out broke. Besides, I'm sure it's nothing I can't fix," I tell her. But the truth is, I should have traded it in for a new model years ago, but the truck holds too many sentimental memories. Hell, it's the truck Blair and I lost our virginity in. It wasn't romantic in the least and looking back, we were both fumbling without a fucking clue, but it meant everything to both of us. I wouldn't change it for the world.

"Then what the hell are you waiting for? Go out there and fix it."

"I'll get right on that," I mutter. "Shall I just pull the tools out of my ass or would you like me to pull them out of yours?"

Blair harrumphs, and I stifle a laugh, having to wipe my hand over my face to hide the smirk lingering on my lips. She didn't seem to approve of the last one I flashed her. "You don't need to be an ass about it," she mutters, crossing her arms over her chest and studiously staring out the window as the heat quickly drains from the truck.

"Who's the one being an ass here? I gave you our options. You're free to walk if you want. It's not like I'm holding you hostage."

Blair groans, clearly frustrated. "I can't . . . I can't be here with you. It's too much."

Her words are like a slap in the face, and I physically draw back. "Wow. Thanks."

She lets out a heavy sigh. "I'm sorry. I didn't mean it like that. It came out all wrong. I just . . . being around you . . . it's hard. Being in this town is hard, but being stuck in your truck with you looking at me like I'm the bane of your existence is killing me."

"Nobody said it was supposed to be easy."

Blair side-eyes me, knowing that's a bullshit line, but I mean, it's all the same. "Besides, you know I get snappy in the cold."

I scoff. "You never could handle it."

"I can too."

"Right, I'll just wait here while you show me how well you can handle it."

"Arghhhhh," she groans, starting to shiver. "You're still the most frustrating human being on the planet."

And she's still the most gorgeous one, but you don't see me screaming it at her.

Her frustration gets the best of her, and she opens the truck door before dropping out onto the snow-covered gravel. "What the fuck are you doing?" I demand, psychically assaulted by the rush of freezing air that crashes through the open door.

Blair leaves the truck door open and starts pacing through the gravel. "Moving," she says, her teeth chattering. "I'm going to get hypothermia if I just sit there for hours on end."

"So this is your grand plan? You're just going to pace until someone decides to drive by?"

"Got any better ideas?"

"I mean, there's always the old fashioned get naked and survive off each other's body heat, but something tells me you're too much of a prude for that."

"Classy," she says. "Tell me, is insulting women until they get naked for you a new personality trait, or one I was just lucky enough to never experience?"

I give her a hard stare. She knows damn well I'm not like that. "Are you fucking kidding me?" I grunt. "I was trying to have fun with you, trying to help you to remove that stick up your ass."

She mutters something under her breath before pausing in the open doorway and fixing her stare on me. "I didn't mean it," she says. "It's the cold."

"Soooo . . . that's a no on getting naked, then?"

"Fucking hell," she says, picking up her pacing right where she left off. "How did my day come to this? I was supposed to spend the rest of the afternoon trying to figure out how to make Christmas feel magical like Nana used to, and then I was going to spend the night drinking while getting the house ready for a fresh paint. But nooooooo. That's too easy, isn't it? Now I'm going to either freeze to death or get mauled by a polar bear."

"A polar bear? Really?"

"Whatever. A grizzly one. I don't think I'll particularly care what kind of bear it is when it's mauling me."

"You're not getting mauled by a bear," I tell her, letting out a heavy sigh, almost having forgotten how ridiculous her rambling can get when she's scared. "If anything, we'll starve and have to fight to the death so one of us can eat the other."

"Great. There's nothing quite like a little cannibalism to get me in the Christmas spirit."

"There you go," I say with a can-do attitude, just shy of giving her the good old thumbs up. "Now you're getting it."

Blair huffs and pulls my coat tighter around her, and for just a split second as the chill seeps into my bones, I regret giving it up, but knowing that she'd be freezing out here has me ready to peel off the rest of my clothes and hand them over too. Hell, I'm starting to think that maybe we should get naked. I hate seeing her freeze.

Her chattering teeth are loud enough to hear across the open cab, and the sound has my hands balling into fists. Hell, keeping myself rooted to my seat is proving to be a challenge when all I want to do is grab her and pull her into me to shock her system for just a moment. I wonder if her blood would start to pump if I kissed her, but not one of those pathetic little pecks, a real fucking kiss that makes her realize exactly what she threw away. All I know is if I keep hearing her shiver, I'll lose any semblance of control.

"What's your plan?" I ask, both of us needing a distraction from the cold.

"Huh?"

"Your plan? For the house? For Blushing? How long are you going to be here?"

"Wow. Trying to get rid of me already?"

I scoff. "Acting as though that's not your main goal is insulting,

Blair. We both know your time here is limited. I just want to know how limited so I can gauge how much damage you're going to cause before you jet out of here and leave me to clean up the mess again."

"Fuck me, Nick," she grunts. "You didn't even pretend to save my feelings on that one."

"Like how you've done for me over the past six years?" I question, arching a brow. "Sucks, doesn't it?"

Her gaze falls away, getting straight back to her shivers when she lets out a sigh, choosing not to dwell on the bullshit. "I don't know how long I'll be here," she finally says. "It really depends how soon I can bring Nana's house into the twenty-first century."

"You're selling it?" I question, though I already know the answer.

"That's the plan," she says. "As for the timing, who knows. Considering the time of year, I'll be lucky if I can source everything I need. Most stores are closing up for the Christmas break, but if I get in quick, I could get most of what I need from Hardin's before John closes up. But accidents happen, and I really have no idea what I'm doing. I had to look up how to patch drywall on YouTube last night, and while it doesn't seem too hard, there are more steps than I realized. I think this renovation is going to take a serious bite out of what little savings I have."

"So, when are you planning on putting it on the market?" I ask, doing what I can not to drop to my knees and tell her that I'll teach her everything she needs to know.

Blair shrugs her shoulders. "I really don't know. I was hoping to get it on the market before Christmas, but Estelle, the real estate agent, let me know I was dreaming. She won't be able to get it listed until mid-January, assuming I've completed everything I need to do. And as for an actual sale, she thinks it could be months."

"Fuck."

"My thoughts exactly," she says. "I need to get out of this place as soon as I can."

Again, her words are like a slap across the face, a shot right through the chest. "Yeah, well fuck you too. Having you back in town wasn't exactly my Christmas wish, but you don't need to go acting as though being in the same area code as me is giving you hives."

"I didn't . . . that's not what I . . . Fuck, Nick. Why do you always have to take everything so personal? I didn't mean I wanted to get out of here because I can't stand being around you. The thought of getting to be in the same damn room as you is the only reason I haven't hightailed it back to New York yet," she says, the cold forcing a little honesty into her words. "I was referring to my new business. I need to get home so I can start figuring out my next steps."

"What are you talking about? What business? You went to New York for your dream job. What happened to that?"

"What do you think happened?" she mutters. "I fucked it up just like I fuck up everything else."

"You got fired?"

She nods, shame flashing in those beautiful blue eyes. "I mean, it's not the first time. My boss and I . . . we don't often see eye to eye, and he certainly doesn't understand my . . . humor. He's fired me a handful of times before, but our clients love me, and every time he lets me go, they've pressured him to bring me back, and I always go willingly. Only this time . . . I don't want to go back."

"So what do you want to do?"

"I'm going to start my own firm," she tells me, sounding somewhat sheepish as though admitting one of her dreams is the hardest thing she's ever done. "My best friend, Rena, is going to help me get off the ground, and I already have a great rapport with my clients from SC Corporate, so considering their current contracts, I think many of them will happily come with me. And I just . . . I don't know. I think I have a good chance of succeeding with this."

"Of course you do," I tell her. "If anybody is going to build a successful business from the ground up and absolutely kill it against the bigwigs in New York, it's you."

Blair presses her lips into a hard line, her gaze falling back to mine. "You really mean that? You're not just saying that because you feel like an ass for saying having me back in town isn't exactly your Christmas wish?"

"I don't feel like an ass for saying that. I was being honest. And yes, I really meant it. I think you can achieve anything you want."

"You really are an ass," she throws back at me, getting catty again, crossing her arms over her chest, pulling the coat even tighter as she picks up her pacing, probably wearing a hole through the ground by now.

I clench my jaw, the cold clearly fucking with my head as I storm out of the truck and stride around the front, goosebumps quickly spreading across my chilled skin. "What the fuck do you want from me, Blair?" I demand, holding my hands out wide. "You want me to lie to you and tell you that seeing you back in town is everything I ever wanted? Because it's not. I've dreamed about bringing you home ever since the day you left, but actually seeing you again is like tearing the wound wide open. You fucking killed me when you left, and I'd give anything not to have to relive that pain again. You think I'm here, getting in your face because I enjoy this? Fucking hell."

I shake my head, running my hands through my cropped hair and turning away from her as I try to find my composure. Then taking a breath, I turn back, meeting her tear-filled stare. "I'm falling apart, Blair. Just the sight of your face is destroying everything I've tried to heal over the past six years, and all you can manage to say is that you can't wait to be out of this godforsaken town. Were you even planning on coming to find me? Did you even care to see where we stood after all these years? Care to see the destruction you left behind?" I take a breath, my hands shaking as I stare into those stunning blue eyes that live in my dreams. "You've come flying back in here without a fucking care of who it impacts, acting as though I'm the one who hurt you, hiding behind counters, and shying away from me as though we weren't part of the same damn whole."

"Don't you fucking get it?" she yells back, the empty roads swallowing the sound of her cries. "I'm ashamed. I'm embarrassed. I fucked up the one amazing thing in my life and have been struggling ever since. Do you have any idea how it feels to have to come back here and face you knowing what I've done? How fucking bad I hurt you. Just seeing you like this, seeing that you're still in pain and knowing that my arrival is making it that much harder is tearing me to pieces."

Tears fall down her cheeks and she hastily wipes them away as she takes a deep, shaky breath, her gaze remaining fixed on mine. "It has never been my intention to hurt you, Nick, because when you hurt, I hurt."

Fuck.

I fall forward, my hands braced against the hood of my truck as my head hangs low, barely able to manage taking in the sound of her heartache and those words I've always needed to hear. Only, I don't know what to do with them or where to go from here. What's the point in knowing that we're both still aching when she's going straight back to New York? Tearing the wound open is all for nothing because, at the end of the day, it's not going to make anything any easier or help me heal and move on. And it sure as fuck doesn't look as though it's helping her.

"So, that's it?" I ask her, unable to even raise my head. "You've said what you needed to say, you'll go back to fixing up your grandparents' place, and then you'll silently slip away when you're done?"

Blair inches toward me, unaware of just how much pain I'm really in. "What's the point, Nick?" she whispers, reaching out toward me before pulling her hand away. "Why dredge up all of these feelings and fuck us both up, only for me to fly back to New York in a few weeks? Doing this, airing all our dirty laundry and putting everything out in the universe isn't helping either of us. It's better this way."

I shake my head, unable to believe the words coming out of her mouth. How could she come back to Blushing thinking she would just sweep it all under the rug and pretend there isn't a gaping hole right in the center of my chest in the shape of her face?

Needing a minute, I turn and walk away, taking a few steps down the quiet road, and I'm grateful when she doesn't try to follow me. Fuck, it feels as though she were leaving me all over again. Only last time, she sat in my lap with her arms wrapped around me, and that somehow managed to soften the blow, but this time, she thrust her fist right into my chest and tore my heart out in one fell swoop before crushing it under her foot like a piece of discarded trash.

When the cold becomes too much, I trail back toward the truck, finding Blair sitting in the back with her stupid tree. She fiddles with something, but I really don't have enough energy to figure out what. Instead, I climb back into the truck before trying the engine as though it might magically work, but God knows I haven't been that lucky today.

The engine fails again, and I lean back in my seat, staring up at the cloudy sky through the dirty windshield. I suppose I should be grateful that it's only a soft snowfall today. It could be worse. There could be a blizzard.

My gaze settles on the rearview mirror, watching Blair as she continues to fiddle, still finding it so surreal that she's even here. I've thought about this moment a million times over, and I can guarantee that it hasn't gone down the way I'd always pictured. Hell, I'm sure Blair's thought about it too.

A deep chill settles into my bones, and I cross my arms over my chest, trying to hold on to what little warmth I have left, wondering just how quickly I'd lose my balls if I suggested Blair get naked in the back of my truck with me. I start searching through my phone for games I can play that don't require cell service when a terrified scream breaks through the silence, the sound like nails on a chalkboard.

"NICK!" Blair screams, the high pitch of her voice tying my stomach in knots.

My head whips up, staring into the rearview mirror to find Blair's tree filled with orange licks of burning flames, quickly spreading. "FUCK!"

Terror grips me in a chokehold, and I bail out of the truck, racing around the side and reaching up toward Blair. With my heart pounding faster than ever before, I grab Blair's arms and yank her back, her body tumbling over the edge of my truck away from the fire as she squeals with fear, but I quickly catch her, barely having a second to help settle her on her feet before reaching for the straps holding the damn tree down. But fuck, there's no denying the heat from the flames is sure as fuck welcome right now.

"No, no, no," Blair panics, looking at the tree she so carefully picked out.

Quickly unstrapping the big bastard, I launch myself up into the bed of my truck and find a portion of the tree that isn't currently burning and throw the fucker down into the freezing snow as smoke billows up into the sky.

"What the fuck, Blair?" I demand, jumping down to the burning tree and kicking up snow over it, hoping like fuck this doesn't turn into some kind of crime scene. I mean, on the bright side, at least all the people in the cemetery are already dead. It's not like we can accidentally kill them again.

A part of me screams to let the tree burn, to let us soak up the warmth it offers, but judging by the look on Blair's face, that suggestion isn't going to go down well. She'd prefer to freeze than to lose the tree she went to all this trouble for.

Blair hurries around to the burning tree, helping me extinguish the flames, and it takes all too long before we're left with a smoking tree, that's now nothing more than singed branches. Well, at least one half of it is. The other half is buried in the snow, so the jury is still out on that.

Blair collapses against my truck, her hand on her chest as she breathes heavily. "Holy shit. I didn't mean for that to happen," she tells me, her eyes wide as her hands shake. She turns around, looking into the bed of the truck and reaching in before pulling out a lighter. "I just . . . I found this in your coat pocket and I was so cold. I was just playing. You know, holding the flame near my face just to feel a little warmth, and I guess the flames caught on the netting around the tree. I'm so sorry. Did you get burned? Are you hurt?"

"I'm fine," I mutter, clenching my jaw. I reach toward her and snatch the lighter out of her hand before she accidentally sets my truck on fire too. Shoving it into my pocket, I glance over the still-smoking tree. "At least this might act like some kind of bat signal. Maybe someone might come looking now."

"Shit," she mutters, moving toward the tree and bending down, trying to pull at a good section of the tree and maneuvering it around to see the other half of it. "I guess this part isn't so bad. It's salvageable, right?"

"Just get a new tree," I tell her.

"Are you kidding? I searched for ages for this tree. It's the only good one they had left. I'm not abandoning it."

"Wow. And here I thought abandoning the things you loved was your specialty."

Blair whirls on me, rage pooling in her eyes, and this time, I know I've crossed a line. "For fuck's sake, Nick? How long are you going to hold it against me? I get it already. I fucked up. I left you. I broke your fucking heart, and it was terrible, but how the hell are your constant string of insults supposed to help? Does talking to me like shit help you feel better? Does it make you feel like the big man on campus? Hell, if I knew you hadn't matured any further than the twenty-three-year-old asshole I left behind, then maybe I would have taken my chances with the frostbite walking home."

"Shit, Blair. I'm sorry," I say, stepping toward her and invading her space, momentarily forgetting that maybe this isn't okay. "It just came out. I'm still so fucking angry at you that I can't seem to reel it in."

"Oh, boo hoo," she spits, shoving her hands against my chest, forcing me back a step. "Stop acting like you're the only one hurting."

Fuck. She's infuriating.

"You walked away from me, remember?" I seethe, stepping into her and forcing her back against my truck, eating up the distance between us. "You were the one who decided on the future of our relationship, not me. You were the one who ended a six-year relationship with nothing more than a half-assed conversation that came out of the fucking blue. You were the one who took off for the big city and decided that what I could offer you here in Blushing wasn't enough. And you, Blair, were the one who couldn't so much as offer me the chance to fight for us. You didn't even ask if I would be willing to come with you. So yeah, I have every fucking right to act any way I want. You. Walked. Away. From. Me."

She breathes heavily, her chest pushing up against mine as silence falls around us, but the tension doesn't break. She holds my stare, the two of us locked in a trance, impossible to look away. My thumb shifts over her knuckles, and before I know it, my other hand is on her waist.

Her lips are only a breath away, right there for the taking, and the way she's looking at me, she knows exactly what I want to do. And damn it, she wants it too.

Blair raises her chin, closing the gap just a little bit more, and I watch as her tongue slips out over her bottom lip. I try to resist, try to tell myself to pull back and walk away, but I'm rooted to the spot, unable to move even an inch when the sound of Oxley's Dukes of Hazzard horn blasts through the silence breaking the trance.

I pull back from Blair, my gaze shifting to Oxley as he hangs out of his window, a stupid grin stretched wide across his face. "Better late than never, right?"

Fucking lovable asshole.

CHAPTER TWELVE
BLAIR

Oxley's truck felt like a million bucks as he drove me home from the airport yesterday, but today, it feels like a prison sentence.

I sit right between Oxley and Nick, my thighs pressed against theirs, and if I weren't in such a foul mood right now, I'd probably be coming up with all the dirty scenarios that could possibly play out in this truck. But unfortunately, Oxley hasn't got the taste for pussy, and as for Nick . . . Well, considering nothing has changed, I'm sure he's not down to share. Perhaps this particular fantasy will have to remain in the confines of my filthy mind.

Oxley hits the gas with my half-singed tree in the back, leaving yet another truck in my wake, while completely unaware of the thick tension between me and Nick. Or if he is, he deserves an Emmy for his performance because he certainly doesn't let on that anything is out of the ordinary.

"Figured you guys needed a hand," Ox says, cranking the heat when he realizes just how cold we are. Though now being pressed right up against Nick, it dawns on me just how kind he was to offer his coat while he froze. His skin is so cold to the touch that it must be painful for him. "Tried both your cells and when it went straight to voicemail, I figured you were either out here fucking in the snow, or something had happened."

"Plenty happened, but there was certainly no fucking in the snow," I tell him, unable to get that moment up against Nick's truck out of my head. Everything changed in that split second. The heat of our argument turned into something wild, and all I could think about was his kiss. If Ox hadn't shown up when he did, maybe there might have been some fucking in the snow.

Oxley laughs and shoves his elbow into my ribs. "You know, if you had just put chains on your tires, none of this would have happened. You'd probably be home with a fully decorated tree, sipping on hot cocoa while doing your best rendition of Mariah Carey's All I Want For Christmas Is You."

I roll my eyes. "If I have to hear about the damn tire chains one more time, I'm going to scream. I get it already. I fucked up. I'm the monster around here. I should have taken a second and figured out how to put the tire chains on."

"Naw, come on. Don't be so hard on yourself. You're not a

monster," Oxley chimes, a smirk stretching across his lips. "You're a fucking bratty devil with a sharp bite, but a monster, you are not."

"I . . . I don't even know how to respond to that."

"It's fine. Stew on it for a few hours and text me your comeback later."

I can't help but laugh as we fly back toward Blushing, reaching the point on the highway where the cell service returns. "Thanks, I think," I say, listening as both mine and Nick's phones start dinging with all of our missed notifications, and I have to admit, I'm surprised by just how many notifications he's getting. Shit, perhaps Rena really did start DMing all his socials with the picture of my new Naughty List.

God. Rena is going to be the death of me one day.

Nick silently fumes beside me, his gaze locked out the window as though he could magically make me disappear if he ignores my presence enough, but his douchiness only has me ready to animatedly tell Oxley about my whole life, making sure to leave Nick out of it while purposefully mixing up details and giving credit for the things he did to other random men. Hmm, I wonder how he'd react if I told Ox how I lost my virginity to Billy McDonald in the back of his pickup. The story is still slightly true. I did lose my virginity in the back of a pickup, only the fuming asshole beside me was the one to have that pleasure.

"Shit, darlin'," Ox continues, not missing a beat, and sure as fuck still oblivious to the tension between me and Nick. Hell, does Oxley not realize how wound up I am by the way Nick's arm brushes against mine, his big, strong thigh sitting right there, begging me to sink my nails into it? "You're lucky my cousin was just finishing up a job. Who knows how long you would have been stuck at that old farm if he couldn't come down and save you."

"I'd hardly call it saving me. He took me from one shitty situation and put me straight into another," I mutter. "Maybe I would have been better off. Who knows? If I got stuck at the Christmas tree farm, Billy's old man might have even invited me in for coffee and I could have stayed in the warmth of their home instead of being stranded on the side of the road with no cell service while being screamed at by my ex for two hours."

"Who knows?" Nick throws back at me. "Maybe if you'd stayed, you would have burned down their whole house and farm instead of just the one tree in the back of my truck."

I resist shoving my elbow into his ribs. "You're impossible."

"And you're a fucking stubborn brat who's incapable of accepting help and being grateful for any that comes your way."

God. I'm going to throttle him in a moment. He knows I'm grateful, but he also knows that I'm far too stubborn to admit it to him. Oxley, on the other hand . . .

I whip around, fixing Oxley with a wide, genuine smile. "Have I mentioned how grateful I am that you came looking for us and saved me? If we had been left there much longer, I'm sure the snow would have eventually taken me whole. Thank you so, so much. I owe you. Whatever you need, all you have to do is ask. Actually, can I offer you a warm meal when we get back to my place? It's the least I can do. But I have to warn you, I'm not the best cook in town, but I'm really good at ordering in."

Oxley grins wide as Nick starts muttering something under his breath. "You know, little lady," Ox says. "As much as I'd love to stay for a bite to eat, in the spirit of surviving my cousin, I'll have to give you a rain check."

I laugh before the sound falls flat. Cousin. That's the second time Oxley has called Nick his cousin, but yesterday as he drove me home from the airport, he'd mentioned that it was only a few months ago he'd helped his cousin bury his aunt. Is he referring to the same cousin?

"Wait," I say, my mind whirling. When we were out by the side of the road, Nick had mentioned something to me about dealing with grief, about how the essence of our loved ones is still around us, woven into the fabric of our memories, and I'd brushed him off, assuming he didn't know what he was talking about because he's never lost anyone in his life, and I was sure that if he had, Nana would have said something. But if I'm right, if Nick is the cousin Oxley was referring to, then his aunt would be Nick's mom. "Oh shit," I breathe, my eyes widening with horror as I grip Nick's hand, looking up into his heavy blue stare.

His brows furrow, clearly having no idea what I've just figured out, but as he holds my stare and takes in the horror deep in my eyes, he quickly figures it out.

"No," I breathe, having so many memories of Nick's mom. Hell, she was practically a mother to me too. Before her, I didn't know what it was like to be loved by a mom. Of course, I always had Nana, but after my real mother abandoned me at six years old, I'd always had a gaping hole in my chest, always wondering what it meant to be loved in that way. Nick's mom gave me that. "I'm so sorry. I didn't—"

"Come on, B," Nick says, fear in his eyes as the grief wells up inside of me, darkening my soul. "After everything that's already gone down today, let's not get into it. I can't talk about her with you, not yet."

I swallow hard. His words are like a blade right through the chest.

"Oh," I say, dropping my gaze and releasing my hold on his hand. I turn my face away, not wanting him to see the fresh tears pooling in my eyes. All of this time, he's been dealing with the loss of his mother, and I've been living it up in New York, blissfully unaware when he needed me more than anything. I wasn't there for him, but when it came down to it, would he have wanted me here in the first place? I doubt it.

I sit in silence, the heaviness stretching between us. My tears start to fall, but in an effort not to draw attention to my grief, I just leave them slowly rolling down my cheeks until they drop to my chest.

With Nick's attention out the window, it's easy to hide my tears, but with my chin pointed toward Oxley, the tears don't entirely go unnoticed. He gives me a small smile, and without skipping a beat, he reaches toward the dash, pressing a button before cranking the volume.

A song begins to play and my brows furrow, recognizing the tune but unable to quite put my finger on it until the line, put your hands down my pants and I'll bet you'll feel nuts blares through the speakers. I burst into an uncontrollable fit of laughter, realizing Oxley has put on only the best song of my childhood, "The Bad Touch" by Bloodhound

Gang.

When the chorus hits, Oxley and I can't resist singing it word for word at the top of our voices while the broody asshole beside me continues to brood, but there's no mistaking the tiny little smirk playing on his lips. He never could resist this song.

The song quickly eats up the tension in the cab, and before I know it, we're flying right back through our little town of Blushing. It's only a few minutes before we pull up outside my nana's place, and knowing that my time with Nick is almost up, a pang of sadness spreads through my chest. I have no idea when I might get to see him again.

Are we just going to leave our insults and admissions hanging in the air around us, with both of us still hurting?

Shit.

Oxley cuts the engine, and before the music has even faded out of existence, Nick's door is open, and he flings himself out into the cold evening air. I hurry after him, positive he's about to dump my tree in the snow and leave me with the task of dragging its singed ass inside, but Oxley's hand on my thigh stops me. "I don't know what you did to that asshole," he mutters. "But you need to fix it. I haven't seen him this worked up since he got that suspension for beating the shit out of Jarrod Sanderson."

I cringe. "I remember that."

Oxley nods. "Then you know just how serious this is."

Fuck.

"I can try, but you know how he is," I say. "Neither of us is in a place where we're capable of having any kind of civilized conversation.

Those two hours stuck on the side of the road were filled with endless screaming back and forth. We—"

"Are you fucking coming?" Nick calls out to Oxley, cutting me off as he unstraps my tree.

Oxley fixes me with a hard stare. "I don't care how you do it," he says, opening his door and glancing back at me. "But you're fixing it. I've got too much going on to have to worry about him too."

"How the hell am I supposed to do that?" I whisper-yell at his back, watching as he climbs out of his truck. "In case you haven't noticed, the guy is impossible."

Oxley whips back around, giving me a stupid grin before reaching into the cab and grabbing his coat. "Sounds like a you problem," he says before bailing and leaving to help Nick with the tree.

I roll my eyes as I scootch out of the truck, and realizing that the boys aren't stopping to dump the tree on the ground, I hurry up ahead of them, leaving footprints in the light smatter of snow coating my driveway. My hand dives deep into my bag, searching for the key, and after way too long, I finally curl my fingers around it.

"Sure, take your time," Nick says impatiently from behind me. "We're only carrying a fucking tree."

I resist turning around and sack-whacking him while his hands are occupied. Instead, I focus on unlocking the door. Screw the Naughty List. I need a fucking drinking list if I'm going to survive being in Blushing for the next few weeks.

Getting the door open, I move out of the way, making space for Nick and Oxley to file through the door with my half-burned tree balanced over their shoulders. They get it situated in the living room, right where Nana always used to put her tree, and I can't help the smile that stretches across my face. Maybe Nick was onto something about feeling the essence of someone within your memories.

The boys are silent as they get the tree secured so it won't fall over and crush me, and as I gaze at the burned remains of the tree, I start to feel that Christmas magic I was searching for. Maybe I was onto something by decorating my home.

Nick stands back and surveys his handiwork before reaching through to the trunk of the tree and rotating it just enough so that the majority of the charred tree is at the back with the luscious green pine needles dazzling at the front. Then just when I expect him to take off, he mutters something to Oxley about starting my fireplace, and before I can tell him that I can figure it out myself, he takes off down the hall.

"Uhhhhh . . . where the hell do you think you're going?" I demand, calling after him as he disappears into my old bedroom.

All I hear are the sounds of Nick moving around, then barely ten seconds later, he storms back out of my room with my old electric heater braced over his big shoulder. Then without another word, he strides out the front door and tosses the heater in the back of Oxley's truck.

"HEY! That's mine."

Nick ignores me, narrowing his gaze as though trying to convince himself not to fire back, and with that, he steps up into the passenger seat of Oxley's truck before the heavy thud of the closing door echoes down the snow-laden street.

Well. That's not exactly how I thought that was going to go down.

Movement behind me catches my attention, and I turn back to find Oxley finishing with the fire, the warmth already beginning to spread through the small cottage home. His gaze lingers out toward his truck, his lips pressed into a hard line.

"Fix it," he says as a reminder, that blueish-gray stare swinging back to me.

Oxley holds my gaze for a moment too long, waiting for a response that I don't want to give. "Okay, fine," I mutter, unsure how one stare from the guy has me ready to cave. "I'll try, but I'm not making any promises. After all, the guy practically gets off on arguing with me."

Oxley scoffs as he walks to my door. "And you don't?" he says, pausing to look back at me.

Shit. He's got me there. Despite how infuriating it's been going back and forth with Nick today, it's also worked me up in a way I haven't felt since . . . Well, since before I left Blushing in the first place.

Not wanting to let on just how right he is, I roll my eyes and scoff. "Whatever," I mutter, following him to the door and taking the handle. I stop there, watching him tromp through the snow, leaving big divots as he makes his way across the yard rather than walking around and using the driveway like a normal human being.

"Look," Oxley says, pausing again to glance back at me. "I have high hopes for you, Blair. You and me, we could really hit it off. You're the perfect bestie I've been searching for. Us together. Hell, girl. We could get up to some real nasty shit, but if you can't figure out your problems with that lump of assholery back there, he's gonna force me to pick a side. And let's face it, he's got a whole lifetime of bullshit that can be used as blackmail to risk getting on his bad side. So I'd really appreciate it if you could just . . . play nice. Hell, maybe even jump his bones if you feel that way inclined. Get him all chuffed up for Christmas. Fuck knows he needs it."

My cheeks flame, and I press my lips into a hard line, refusing to respond to any of that because . . . how? The thought of climbing into Nick's bed and riding him like a freaking cowgirl has haunted all of my most delicious thoughts, but actually doing it? Shit. I can't afford to allow myself to hope like that. Nick and I always had the most sizzling chemistry when it came to sex. We worked so well together, and there was never a time when I was left wanting. He knew exactly how to please me, and God, I've been searching high and low for someone who could make me feel like that again, but it's an impossible task. Nobody will ever make me come alive the way Nick did.

My gaze remains locked on Oxley's truck, just waiting for Nick to glance back at me, even only for a second, but he never does, and before I know it, Oxley is seated behind the steering wheel and hitting the gas, taking my heart right along with him as the boys disappear down the street.

Knowing if I dwell on it too much, the rest of my night will be spent crying on the sofa, so I put it to the back of my mind, hoping that at some point over the next few weeks, Nick might offer me the chance to sit down with him and talk it out like we both clearly need.

Wanting to keep myself busy, I trudge through the snow, heading out toward the shed, my body already starting to sweat at the mere idea of having to walk in there, but luckily, my afternoon with Nick has left me so worked up that I might just have the balls to actually get further than the door.

My nerves reach an all-time high, and I remind myself that I was a badass lumberjack today, and if the shed monster wants to come for me, then I'll happily show him the new tricks I learned with a saw. I get the door open, and with the remaining sunlight, I'm able to quickly find Nana's old tubs of Christmas decorations. She always went hard when it came to turning our home into a winter wonderland, and I'm not going to lie, I'm slightly horrified by the mounds of tubs staring back at me. But I can manage . . . right?

Shit.

Realizing these old tubs aren't going to move themselves, I start digging them out while repeating over and over again that the shed monster isn't real. I drag them out onto the snow-covered grass, and the minute they're all out, I hastily shut the shed doors, not having realized that my whole body is covered in a sheer layer of nervous sweat.

I try to calm myself as I drag the heavy tubs toward the door, and just as I grab the final one, a small blue hatchback pulls to a stop outside my home.

I pause, my brows furrowed as I watch the car door open, and when a familiar head of hair steps out into the chilly evening, carrying not one, but four bottles of wine, a cheesy-as-fuck grin stretches across my face.

Sarah grins right back. "News of your afternoon is spreading through town like wildfire," she says, grabbing one of the bottles by the neck and holding it up as she trudges up the driveway. "Figured you need a few of these."

"Oh, thank God," I sigh with relief, all but dropping to my knees.

"Did you really have to abandon two separate trucks and get stranded on the side of the road for an hour?"

"Two hours," I tell her, immediately pulling her into my arms for a big hug the moment she reaches the porch. "Without heating, and with a broody asshole who insisted on dredging up the past."

"Oh shit. Good thing I brought more than one bottle."

"You have no idea how happy I am to see you."

Sarah smiles wide before waltzing straight through the front door. "I'll pour the wine," she calls over her shoulder. "You bring those tubs in, and I'll find the Christmas tunes. Then we can get fucked up decorating and talking shit about Nicholas Stone."

Warmth spreads through my chest, and I grab the tub on top, following her in. "It's like music to my ears."

CHAPTER THIRTEEN
NICK

It's been four long-ass days since Blair returned home to Blushing, and every minute of those four days has been nothing but a nightmare for me.

Okay, maybe I'm exaggerating just a little bit, but for the first time in six long years, I'm starting to feel hope, and that's what's causing me this insane grief. Hope is dangerous, and fuck, I've already watched her walk away once. I sure as hell won't survive it again. And that right there is why having her back home is a nightmare.

Fuck. I love her.

Ever since I took off with her electric heater, I haven't been able to stop replaying that afternoon in my head. The words we threw at each other, each one of them filled with venom, were a hard pill to swallow. I said things I probably wouldn't have had we been capable of talking like mature adults, and I'm sure she admitted to things she wasn't ready to say. But in the grand scheme of things, all that matters is that she's still hurting.

Fuck my feelings, fuck my pain. I can handle them, but what I can't handle is knowing that she's spent the last six years in agony. It kills me.

All this time, I thought she was living it up in New York, happy as a fucking clam as she made leaps and bounds in her career. Last I'd heard from Olivia, Blair was dating some big-time lawyer and living in her expensive city apartment. But what fucks with my head is if she had all of that, everything she wanted, everything she left me for, then why the hell is she still hurting?

She told me that leaving Blushing and walking away from me was the biggest mistake she's ever made, and those words haven't stopped playing on repeat in my head. If she felt that way, then why the hell didn't she come home sooner? Why didn't she pick up the fucking phone and call me? Because she has no fucking intention of being with me, that's why. She's hell-bent on heading back to New York and starting her new business. She doesn't give a shit about the destruction she'll leave behind . . . again.

Some things never fucking change.

I drive through the main street of Blushing, doing what I can to focus on anything but Blair, but as I pass the local coffee house and see Frank's tow truck parked out front, I'm reminded of her all over again. I spent yesterday back at the Christmas tree farm with Frank and Oxley trying to figure out how the fuck we were going to get the old pickup out of the ditch, and after four agonizing hours and an almost-broken leg, the truck was freed. It still worked like a charm, and after dropping it back at Blair's place and leaving the key in the plant on the porch, I received a simple text from Blair with one lone word—thanks.

I tried not to hold it against her. After all, news had gotten around that Sarah and Blair had reunited after all these years over a few bottles of wine. Apparently, after deafening the whole street with their Christmas caroling, decorating the house, and making snow angels, they both passed out. And if Blair still reacts the same to alcohol as she did when she was in her early twenties, then she would have spent the majority of yesterday hungover and feeling sorry for herself. On the other hand, I'm glad she got a chance to hang out with Sarah again. They were tight in high school, and they always brought out the best in each other. Hell, maybe a good solid friendship might just be something that could convince her to stay . . . if only for a little while longer.

Shit. There I go getting all hopeful again.

The rest of my day was spent lying on my cold driveway beneath the engine of my truck after Frank so kindly towed it back to my place, but just as I thought, my old truck—along with the memories it holds—isn't out for the count yet. She'll live to see another day.

Continuing down the street, I pull into the parking lot of Hardin's Hardware and make my way inside. This time of year, I haven't got much to work on . . . at least until after Christmas. Right now, people are spending all their hard-earned cash on Christmas presents, but as soon as Christmas is done and everyone is stuck at home with nothing to do, they'll turn to home renovations. That's when my phone will start blowing up.

Walking through the door of Hardin's Hardware, I find John crouched behind the counter, searching through a bunch of old receipts and looking scrambled. "What have you got for me?" I ask, referring to the message I got last night and bracing a hand against the counter, looking over the mess he's making.

John shakes his head, not able to focus on so many things at the same time. Eventually he looks up from the receipts and glances at me as if only now just realizing I'm standing right in front of him. "Oh, Nick. How're you doing today?"

A grin cuts across my face. "I'm good. What about you? Need a hand?"

"Oh no. Just misplaced some paperwork," he says, reaching for his appointment book. "I'm sure it'll show up eventually."

"No doubt," I agree, despite knowing it's a lost cause. John has been misplacing paperwork since the day he was handed the keys to the castle.

He fumbles around with the appointment book, trying to find today's page. "A young woman was in yesterday," he starts. "Said something about renovating her nana's house."

My stomach drops. Don't fucking tell me he's scheduled me to work for Blair today.

"Ahh, here it is," he says, flipping to the right page. "The backdoor isn't locking properly and the kitchen window is getting jammed. She wanted to fix them herself and needed some guidance on how to do it, but I said not to worry, that I'll send someone out to help her."

"Oh great."

"Wonderful," he says, scanning through his notes. "Now, she's down on—"

"I got it," I mutter. "The old Wilder residence."

"Yes, that's the one," he chuffs. "We got to chatting. She's Olivia and Roy's granddaughter back in town for Christmas, and she's fixing up the place to sell in the new year. Looks like she'll be needing quite a bit of help over the next few weeks."

Just fucking great.

Letting out a heavy sigh, I run my hand back through my hair and consider just how hard it would be to build a rocket and shoot my ass out of here, but then the thought of leaving Blair with an unlockable backdoor and a jammed window makes me sweat. While the crime rate in Blushing is low, it's not exactly zero, and I'd never forgive myself if something happened to her because I'd avoided making her home safe.

"Alright, I'll head over there now," I tell him, knowing he's waiting for some kind of confirmation that I'll take the job, otherwise, he would have trudged out there after he closed up this afternoon.

"Very good," he says, watching me as I stride back out of the shop. I get to the door, and just as I go to push my way out, his voice cuts through the silence. "Oh, and Nick?" he calls out. "She's a pretty young thing. Might be worth getting to know the girl while she's in town."

Fucking hell.

I give John a tight smile. "Always looking out," I say, appreciating his effort, but in this particular case, it's really not required. "I'll take it under advisement."

"Atta boy," he says with a grin that's the equivalent of a pat on the back.

Needing to get out of here before he starts explaining how to ask her out and the meaning of the birds and the bees, I take off and get back into my truck, mentally going over everything I'll need to fix the lock and window and trying to keep my mind off the fact that I'm about to walk back into the home that holds so many memories.

This couldn't possibly go wrong.

Ten minutes later, I pull up outside Blair's home, and as I step out of my truck, I've never felt such dread in my life. I've been studiously ignoring this part of town—apart from dropping her truck home yesterday—simply to avoid having another screaming match with Blair. Don't get me wrong, getting her so worked up that she physically can't control herself gives me life, but it's not what either of us needs.

Making my way up the drive, I can't help but notice that it needs to be shoveled again. We've had steady snowfall over the past few days, but not enough to keep us all locked indoors. I wonder just how hot her blood would boil if I were to do it again. Would she have the guts to come and bust my balls for it, or would I get another lousy text like yesterday? Thanks.

If there's one thing I know about Blair, it's that she always needs to have the last word, and sending that one-word text would have driven her insane, but the fact that she did it in that way . . . well shit, that drove me insane and she damn well knows it.

Lifting my hand, I knock on the door before I convince myself to turn around, and before I can even finish knocking, she tears the door open, her eyes already narrowed on me as if knowing exactly who stood on the other side. "What are you doing here?"

"Your backdoor isn't locking and your window is jammed. I'm here to fix it."

Her eyes widen with horror. "You?"

"Who else would it be? The fucking Grinch?"

Blair scoffs, more than agreeing, but she sure as fuck doesn't move out of the way, and I let out a heavy sigh. "You want it fixed or not?"

"What other options do I have?"

I shrug my shoulders, purposefully not making any of her options sound very enticing, because let's face it, I want to be inside that house. I want to be in her space. "You could wait for John to have time. Could be a week. Could be two. You could do it yourself, but let's be honest, we know how that's going to go. Or you could swallow your fucking pride and step out of the way so I can get it over and done with."

Blair clenches her jaw, clearly not thrilled with her current predicament. "Fine," she finally huffs out.

I grin wide, and as she steps back, making space for me to pass, I welcome myself into her home before immediately coming to a halt. "Why the fuck is it freezing in here?" I ask, my gaze quickly sweeping the house and noticing the bed made up right in front of the dwindling fire. But hell, I almost missed it among the Christmas spirit that's violated the house. There's tinsel, bells, garlands, and glitter spread from one end of the house to the other. Not gonna lie though, she's done an incredible job.

"I uhh . . ." she pauses, cringing as she kicks the door shut behind me.

"Spit it out, Blair."

"Ugh," she groans, storming to the kitchen to point out the jammed window that's now not so much jammed, but non-existent. "It got jammed yesterday when I opened it, and then I tried to fix it last night, and now it's . . ." Her words fade away as her gaze drops to the floor by the dining table to where the whole fucking window is propped up against the chair leg.

"How the fuck—you know what? I don't want to know," I say, striding deeper into the kitchen to look over the window, hoping like fuck it's an easy fix. "Why did you need to open the window in the first place? It's the middle of winter."

"I was sanding the walls and the house was getting all stuffy."

"You were what?" I grunt, my head snapping up from the window to take in the walls, only horror blasts through my chest at the sight. "Fuck, B. You didn't sand the walls, you massacred them."

"What are you talking about?" she demands, looking over her work. "I did a great job. There were holes and little cracks everywhere."

"Yeah, but now the walls are wavy," I tell her. "Look from the side. You've sanded it so hard, you've created divots in the wall."

"What?" she groans, moving across the kitchen to look at the wall from a new angle, and the moment she does, her shoulders droop with defeat. "Shit."

"It's fine. I can fix it," I murmur, her defeat singeing my very soul.

Despite everything, despite the hurt and ugliness of the last six years, I've never wanted her to fail.

She lets out a heavy sigh before dropping into one of the dining table chairs, her elbows braced on the table as she hangs her head into her hands. "I am way out of my league here," she says.

"No shit. You're a big-city girl who doesn't like to get her hands dirty. You're not the DIY type," I say as I grip the window on either side and lift it onto the counter, trying to judge just how hard this is going to be to fix. "But having said that, you're also the kind of girl who can do anything she puts her mind to. You just need a little guidance first."

Blair lifts her head, her brow arching as she meets my gaze. "Are you offering?"

I press my lips into a hard line, really not knowing the answer to that. Instead, I nod toward the mess of blankets piled up in front of the fireplace. "You slept out there?"

"Mm-hmm," she says. "Some asshole stole my electric heater, and with the window out, the house turned into a freaking igloo. I had to set an alarm and wake up every hour to put more wood on the fire, otherwise, I would have frozen."

I gape at her. "And you didn't think to call me?"

"Oh, I definitely thought about it, but in the end, I chose my pride over my survival instincts. If I knew you were going to be the one showing up today, maybe I would have reconsidered," she muses. "Actually . . . no, I wouldn't have. I was happy freezing."

I scoff as I reach for my tools. "You really hate me that fucking much?"

"What?" she breathes, her eyes widening. "Is that what you think? That I hate you?"

I let out a heavy breath. "Honestly, I have no fucking idea what I think, and when it comes down to it, I don't think you do either."

She visibly swallows, her gaze dropping back to the table. "I've never hated you, Nick," she whispers, getting to her feet. "I, ummm . . . I've got a lot to do if I'm going to get the house painted before Christmas."

Blair quickly excuses herself from the kitchen, disappearing into one of the spare bedrooms, and just as I turn my attention back to the window, Christmas carols blast through the house.

I blow out a heavy breath. I'm all for the people of Blushing getting into the Christmas spirit and shitting baubles, but Christmas music has always been like nails on a chalkboard to me.

Doing my best to ignore the screechy song coming from down the hall, I go about my business getting the window installed back into the frame and fixing the parts of the frame that are keeping it jammed. The second the window is back to its former glory, the warmth begins spreading through the house again, and a hear a relieved, "Thank fuck," from down the hall.

I move on to the backdoor, noticing a few issues around the house that weren't added to the multiple to-do lists Blair has stuck to the fridge, and I make a mental note to add them when I wander back out there.

The backdoor lock is a fucking bitch and takes much longer than anticipated, and when I walk back out to grab a different tool, I find Blair padding around the kitchen, in the middle of dishing up two plates, one with a half turkey sub and the other nearly overflowing.

I arch my brow as she turns around, pausing when she notices me standing by the dining table. "Oh, umm . . . I made you lunch. Figured you might be hungry."

I'm overcome by shock, and not knowing how to respond, I just stare, and her expression quickly morphs. "For fuck's sake, Nick. It's not like I poisoned it. It's just a turkey sub. If you don't want it, that's fine. I'll throw it in the trash. Doesn't matter to me if you'd prefer to starve."

She goes to reach for the plate and I quickly step in, taking it from her hand. "Woah. No need to be hasty," I say. "I was just . . . surprised. After the way things ended the other day, I figured the next time you saw me, you'd come armed with killer pinecones."

"Consider it a peace offering," she tells me, glancing toward the table and going to make a move toward it before thinking better of it and remaining by the kitchen counter. "But really, if I had poisoned it, could you blame me? You were an ass."

"You weren't exactly an angel, either."

"I know. I'm sorry," she says. "I've pictured the moment we'd see each other again a million times over, and it never went like that."

"Oh yeah?" I ask, placing my plate down on the dining table and moving across the kitchen, placing myself right in front of her, her chest grazing mine. "And how exactly did you picture it going down?"

Blair's cheeks flush, and she purposefully takes a too-big bite of her sub, rendering her unable to speak, not without spitting turkey from one end of the kitchen to the other. And despite being more than prepared to wait her out, somehow I feel that I'll never get the answer to that question.

A smirk stretches across my lips, and I lean into her, watching the way she sucks in a breath, her chin lifting as if waiting for me to close the gap. And fuck, I've never wanted something more, but instead of giving in to my every desire and kissing her, I reach around her and take the pen that's been left haphazardly on the counter. "Your laundry sink is leaking," I tell her, pinching the corner of one of her many to-do lists and tearing it off the fridge. "You're gonna need someone to take care of those pipes for you."

Blair blanches, and I give her a moment to recover as I scrawl laundry sink at the bottom of the list. I get back to my sub as Blair cleans up the kitchen, stealing my plate out from under me and dumping it into the sink before I've had a chance to finish my lunch.

She trails out of the kitchen and I find myself following her down the hall to the spare room she'd been working in earlier. It's practically an empty canvas, the furniture all pushed into the center of the room and draped with old sheets while the walls bear evidence of her handiwork.

"So, you're really selling this place, huh?" I ask, leaning against the doorframe, watching as she scoops out some wall putty and slathers it across the wall, doing what she can to patch up the wear and tear of the last fifty years.

"I don't want to," she says, slathering way too much putty onto the wall. "But what choice do I have? I want to build this new business, and while I have enough to get started, it's not enough to support me while the business grows and develops. It's my only safety net."

"Yeah, I get it," I say, mirroring that same defeat Blair showed when she realized she put a wave in the wall. She really has her heart set on heading back to New York and starting her next chapter, but why should it bother me? I came to the realization that she has her big-city life and that a small-town guy like me has absolutely nothing to offer her.

She's forever going to be the one who got away, even now when she's standing right in front of me.

I watch her for a second longer before I run out of control and step deeper into the room. "You're doing it wrong." Stepping in behind her, I take the small spatula out of her hand and show her how much putty she needs to scoop before demonstrating the best way to smooth it onto the wall. She watches me with a keen eye, taking everything in and slowly nodding. Then simply because I can't help myself, I scrape off the excess putty from her previous attempts and start making my way around the room. "If you've got too much product, you'll be waiting too long for it to dry before you can start sanding. You won't be painting for days."

Blair lets out a frustrated huff before leaning back against the door. "I'm never going to get the hang of this."

"You will," I encourage, and once every last defect in the wall has been filled, I put the spatula down and walk out of the room, knowing that if I spend one more second in here, I won't be able to resist falling to my knees and begging her to take me back.

CHAPTER FOURTEEN
BLAIR

Sitting in the park where Nana used to take me as a young girl, I watch as the late afternoon turns into night. It's exactly six days before Christmas, and I've never felt so lost. It's been a big few days preparing the house for renovations, but instead of feeling hopeful or accomplished, I feel like a hamster on a wheel, perpetually running a race I have no hope of winning.

If I could hold on to Nana and Pop's house for the rest of my life, I would. But even if I didn't need the money, it's only right that the house be sold to someone else. Perhaps a young family that's just starting their lives together. Perhaps this could be their first home where they will welcome their children and make memories. Perhaps the couple would grow old in that home the same way Nana and Pop did, and they would cherish it with everything they are.

That's the dream right there.

As for me, I'm suddenly finding myself wondering if my dream of starting a new business in New York is really what I want.

Seeing Nick again and having him in my space the other day was a lot to take in. We weren't fighting, weren't trying to invoke some kind of war, we were just being, and damn it, I hate how nice it was. But when he stepped into me by the kitchen counter, I could have sworn he was going to kiss me, and at that very moment, I couldn't breathe. Just like out on the side of the road, but that was different, that was full of ravenous emotion. In the kitchen when he looked into my eyes and I could feel his warmth enveloping me, I could have crumbled. Hell, I would have been a puddle on the ground if he'd actually closed the gap and pressed those full lips against mine.

"I need help, Nana," I whisper into the night, gazing up at the moonlight that spreads a beautiful glow over Blushing. "I need you to tell me what to do. I've never felt so lost. I'm a mess. I love being home in Blushing, but I hate that the reason I'm here is because you're gone. You brought me here and forced Nick back into my life, and now the thought of having to leave him behind again is already haunting me. I can't bear to hurt him again."

Tears well in my eyes, and I try to blink them back. "Please, Nana. Send me a sign. Tell me what I'm supposed to do."

Leaning forward on the small park bench, I brace my elbows against my knees, and just as I hang my head down into my hand, a bright flash of light steals my attention. I gaze down the street, trying to figure out what the hell I'm looking at when I realize it's a neon sign that reads OPEN in the window of Blushing's most beloved Bar & Grill.

Oh, thank God. I don't mind if I do.

Getting up from the bench, I take my time as I stroll through the familiar streets of Blushing, and by the time I push through the door, I've got a message from Sarah saying she's already on her way.

Making my way through the busy bar, I find a stool right at the bar and make myself comfortable, arching a brow as I find my new bestie, Oxley, busily pouring a drink.

"Well, shit," he says, a smirk playing on his lips as he puts a beer down on the bar and slides it toward an eager customer. "Something tells me this might just be the best night I've ever had behind this bar."

"Oxley Stone, what the hell are you doing working here?" I ask. "I thought you worked out by the airport doing . . . actually, I have no idea what you do."

Oxley laughs and reaches for a wine glass. "That ring didn't pay for itself, you know?" he says, indicating toward the chilled bottles behind him. "I take it you're a Moscato girl?"

I scoff, silently surprised by how well he was able to read me. I'm absolutely a Moscato girl, but tonight, I'm gonna need something a little stronger. "Usually I am," I admit. "But I'm here to get fucked up."

"Ahhh, say no more." Oxley abandons the wine glass before grabbing a bunch of mixers, and before I can even think about what I want, he places the perfect concoction in front of me. "That should do the trick," he says with a devastatingly gorgeous wink.

Narrowing my gaze on the glass, I drag it toward me before lifting it to my lips and taking a small pull from the straw, and my mouth instantly fills with sinful bliss. "Holy shit," I groan, taking a deeper pull. "Are you sure you're really into dudes? This is so freaking good. I'll marry you if he says no."

"Right. Because Nick is really going to stand for that," he says. "Tell me, have you fixed it yet?"

My phone rings on the bar, and I grin at Oxley. "Ahh, would you look at that? Saved by the bell."

He rolls his eyes, and my mood immediately plummets finding Dwayne's name, my boss from SC Corporate Management, flashing across my screen. I knew he'd come crawling back. It was only a matter of time.

I consider ignoring the call, really not wanting to deal with his bullshit tonight, but I also can't resist the opportunity to hear him beg and grovel and tell me how much he fucked up. So despite my better judgment, I accept the call and press the phone to my ear.

"Dwayne," I say in greeting, letting him hear the venom in my tone.

"Blair, hey," he says, hesitation thick in his voice. "Listen, I know you and I have had our differences over the years, but the clients want you back. So, I'm willing to look past your donkey meme and the bullshit defamatory email that followed if you'd be happy to return. There would need to be consequences for the email blast, but I think we can work past them."

I laugh. "You're kidding, right?"

"Don't make this harder than it needs to be, Blair. We both know that you're going to come back. You love your position here. Just cut to the chase and tell me what it's going to take to get you back."

"I told you when I left," I say, noticing the way Oxley watches me a little too closely. "I'm never coming back. I'm better on my own. I'm standing by everything I said. You screwed me over far too many times. So now it's my turn."

"Quit bullshitting me, Blair."

"Woah. Quite the attitude for someone who's desperate to get me back."

Oxley leans in closer, his gaze narrowed on mine with a deep suspicion. "Do you have a boyfriend over in New York that Nick should know about? You're not about to screw him over again."

"Fuck no," I say, interrupting Dwayne's fuming. "It's my old boss. He fired my ass and now the company is pressuring him to bring me back because I'm the best senior publicist the company has ever had and the clients will walk without me. Just as I predicted. Isn't that right, Dwayne?"

Dwayne huffs and puffs. "Fuck you, Blair. You're only making it harder for yourself. You know you can't compete against SC, and the bigwigs upstairs aren't going to accept your bullshit for long, especially when you start poaching clients and affecting their profit margins. You'll be blacklisted in this industry."

A smile flitters across my lips. "What's the matter, Dwayne? You sound scared."

"Come on, Blair. My ass is on the line here," he finally admits with a heavy resignation. "The clients want you back. Otherwise, they're walking. Just tell me your terms so we can get on with it. I'll even reinstate your Christmas bonus."

"Take your Christmas bonus and shove it up your ass. I'm not coming back. I'm starting my own firm, and if every single one of your clients chooses to sign with me, then so be it. But it won't be because I poached them, it'll be because they know who the best person is to represent them. Time to face the music, Dwayne. You got your position because you have a dick, not because you're good at what you do, and it's not my fault that the clients have finally figured out that you have no idea what you're doing."

"Blair—"

"Good luck, Dwayne. You're gonna need it."

I end the call, a cheesy grin resting on my face.

Fuck that felt good.

Oxley refills my glass and arches a brow, far too curious about what just went down to be innocent, though something tells me he's just looking out for Nick. But he doesn't need to worry about that because Nick and I are well and truly over . . . I think.

"So, that's what sticking it to the man looks like, huh?"

"I mean, I prefer when a big burly man sticks it to me, on my knees with my head slammed down into the mattress. And while that definitely doesn't compare to a good, thorough pounding, it was thrilling all the same."

"Eww. I just know you were thinking about my cousin when you said that."

A wicked smirk stretches across my face. I'm not going to deny it. Nick and I always had the best chemistry between the sheets. I laugh and grab my drink, taking a long pull from the straw. "So, speaking of the ring that didn't pay for itself," I say, shifting the topic faster than I changed my sheets after the thought of my asshole ex, Marc, screwing around in them with his mid-afternoon snack. "Are you nervous?"

Oxley seems to silently laugh at me, probably realizing exactly what I'm doing. "Shitting my pants," he says with a charming smirk, his eyes lighting up like Christmas morning. "You're going to be there, right?"

My jaw drops, and I gape at Oxley, warmth spreading through my stone-cold chest. "Me? Really? I wouldn't miss it for the world, but are you sure? I wouldn't want to intrude."

"I wouldn't ask if I wasn't sure," he says, busily moving around the bar. "Besides, something tells me you'll be sticking around for a little while. Not to mention, between you and me, it's not like you have any other plans anyway. Unless you were particularly fond of your current plan to spend your Christmas Eve sulking alone at home like the miserable little loner that you are."

"Ouch!"

"Try and tell me I'm wrong." He arches a brow, his hand pausing over the bar to fix me with a challenging stare—a challenge I know I would lose every day of the week.

I roll my eyes. We both know he's right, but admitting it feels like a crime against myself. I'm saved by the bell as Sarah strides through the doors with a wide grin across her face, looking more than ready to let off a little steam.

"Ahhhh. I stand corrected. Perhaps you're not a miserable little loner after all," Oxley chimes, already working on a drink for Sarah as though knowing her order like it's permanently etched into his brain. A teasing smirk dances on his lips. "Perhaps you're a miserable little couple."

"Hey," Sarah says, dropping down beside me at the bar. "I heard that."

"You were meant to," Oxley laughs, sliding her drink toward her like the perfect bartender.

Sarah lets out a huff, her gaze swinging toward me. "I've had the worst freaking day," she says, lifting her glass to her lips, bypassing the straw, and drinking straight from the rim. Actually, drinking is the wrong word. It's more like a desperate chug. The half-empty glass is put back on the bar, and she takes a breath, having to wipe the sides of her lips clean. "Do you have any idea how stupid some people can be? It's Blushing. Our hospital is supposed to be nearly empty, but the second the snow rolled in, it's as though people's brain cells got frozen along with it."

Sarah launches into the rundown of her day, and I smile and laugh along with her stories before she throws the limelight onto me, and I go into vast detail about how well I've managed to avoid Nick over the last few days. I tell her about our lunch together in my kitchen and how effortless it felt, and by the time my cheeks have finished flushing at the very thought of him, we're both drunk.

Oxley becomes our designated server for the night, keeping a close eye on us as other bar-goers try to shamelessly hit on us, but hell, if they're willing to buy us a few drinks, I'm willing to spend their money.

We outlast nearly everyone in the bar, and it's not until a familiar scent assaults my senses and my skin becomes hyper-aware of the man standing behind me that my gaze shoots up to Oxley's in accusation. "You called the fun police?"

"No," he says. "You called him."

My face scrunches. Surely he's lying because I know without a doubt that I wouldn't have called that grumpy-ass. But then, maybe I would.

Sarah's face twists with confusion, clearly having no idea what I've already sensed behind me. As she turns, her face quickly morphs into horror. "Oh noooo," she groans, her head having to tilt back just to meet his stare. She nudges me with her elbow, just in case I haven't noticed him, before leaning toward me, blinking rapidly as though trying to blink him out of existence. "I think Nick is here. Or maybe he's not. I think there's two of him." She leans forward, almost tumbling off her barstool as she takes a deep breath, sniffing him, and if it weren't for Nick catching her and pushing her back, she'd already be on the dirty ground. "Shit, B. He smells good. I wonder if he fucks as good as he smells."

A lazy grin stretches across my face, remembering it all so damn well. "Oh, he does."

Feeling his heated stare shift toward me, I risk meeting his eyes, and damn it, that was the biggest mistake I've ever made. The way he's looking at me right now, all dominating and filled with intense hunger, I'm at risk of dropping to my knees right here.

My tongue rolls over my bottom lip, and I can't help but reach toward him, my fingers grazing over the front of his shirt, feeling the defined ridges of his abs below. "Hmmmm. I've missed you," I say, jumping up from the barstool and having to fist my fingers into the material of his shirt to keep from swaying. "Why don't we head out to that truck of yours and I'll show you just how much I've missed you?"

Nick's deep blue eyes seem to penetrate mine and dive right down into my soul before he cuts our connection and glances toward Oxley. "Just how fucking drunk are they?"

Oxley grins. "You don't wanna know the answer to that."

"Shit."

Nick's hand finds my waist before sliding right around to my back, holding me close to his chest before glancing at Sarah. "Come on," he says to her, offering a hand to keep her steady. "Get in my truck."

My eyes widen, snapping up to Nick's. "Oh. I didn't realize you were into sharing," I slur, gripping his strong arm, my fingers slowly working their way up and around the back of his neck. "I mean, it'll be a tight fit for the three of us, and I can't promise that I won't get jealous, but if that's what you really want . . ."

I let the words hang between us, and Nick looks at me as though I've just lost my mind. "Fucking hell, Blair. I don't want to fuck either of you in the back of my truck. I'm driving your asses home before you end up passed out in the street."

At the mention of the street, my gaze flicks out the window, looking past Nick's red pickup parked just outside the door and to the light dusting of snow covering the road. "Oh," I gasp, my stare meeting Sarah's. "I haven't made snow angels in years."

Her eyes widen like saucers. "Uhhh . . . Pretty sure we might have made snow angels the other night, but YES! Absolutely! Let's do it."

Nick shakes his head. "Great idea. Let's all go and lay down in the middle of the road and make fucking angels." His sarcasm isn't lost on me, and as his heated stare comes back to mine, I cringe. "Get in the fucking truck, Blair. Don't make me have to put you in there, because you know I will."

That lazy smile returns to my lips, remembering just how strong he is, and my fingers trail back down to those delicious biceps. "Do you only like to throw me around when I'm being a brat, or do you just like putting your hands on me? Because if that's the case, I know a few things you could do with your—"

"Blair," he roars, cutting me off. "Get your sweet ass in my truck right fucking now."

"Oooh," Sarah says, watching the way he gets all worked up. "I think I like this new grumpy version of Nicholas Stone. It's tantalizing."

I snicker at the word tantalizing, because let's face it, it's a funny word, and the way it slurs from Sarah's lips somehow only makes it that much better.

Nick groans, reaching over me to grab both mine and Sarah's purses from the bar before scooping his arm further around my back, putting me by his side. He shoves our purses under his arm before putting Sarah at his other side and leading us both out of the bar, but I can't help looking back over my shoulder and grinning at Oxley. "Bye, friend. It has been my pleasure serving with you tonight."

"Bitch, you didn't serve shit," he chuckles, shaking his head.

"Oh, I served," I tell him, having absolutely no idea what I'm talking about. "You just don't know it yet."

Nick mutters something under his breath and continues to drag Sarah and me out into the cold and over to his truck. He helps Sarah into the backseat before taking my hand and leading me around to the passenger side, and it doesn't go unnoticed just how often his skin grazes mine. Hell, I'm left with goosebumps everywhere he's touched me.

Just as it always is, the tension thickens between us in the cab as he drives Sarah home, and when we're finally left alone, it's almost impossible to ignore.

My hands ball into fists, and I have to force them under my thighs to keep myself from reaching out to him, but damn, if he gave me even the slightest indication that he was down for it, I'd climb him like a damn tree.

Pulling up at my place, Nick gets out and helps me up the slippery driveway, muttering something about being an idiot who hasn't shoveled it yet, despite my declaration that I can take care of myself.

When I fumble for my keys, Nick takes my purse and finds them for me, unlocking the door and opening it wide. He ushers me inside, and just when I expect him to close the door behind me, he follows me in, bringing that tension right along with him.

"What are you doing?" I ask in a small tone.

"Making sure you get to bed without killing yourself," he says, stopping by the kitchen and fishing painkillers out of my cupboard before filling a glass of water. He turns back to face me, his brows furrowed as he finds me watching him. "What are you waiting for?" he asks, nodding toward the hallway that leads to the bedrooms. "Go."

Oooh, it seems I have cranky Nick tonight. It's kinda sexy.

Making my way down the hall, I brace my hand against the freshly painted walls, keeping myself upright, and when I move into my bedroom, Nick walks straight in behind me, putting the painkillers and water onto my bedside table.

He grabs the corner of my blanket and flings it back, clearly ready to tell me to get my ass into bed, only the movement has everything that was on my bed flying off, leaving my bright pink vibrator to drop heavily to the ground between us.

I cringe, humiliation flooding through me. "Any chance you didn't see that?" I ask, looking anywhere but at the vibrator or his eyes.

"Oh, I definitely see it."

Shit. Though . . . it's not like I'm one to throw away a perfectly good opportunity when it smacks me in the face.

My gaze shifts up, meeting those blue-gray eyes that have lived in my memory for far too long, and I lower my tone to a breathy whisper, my tongue rolling over my bottom lip as heat builds between my thighs. "Then what are the chances you'd like to see exactly what it is I do with it?"

Nick swallows, his Adam's apple gently bobbing up and down his throat. As he steps closer, his warm hand grazes my waist, and my knees weaken. I try to catch my breath, but the tension makes it impossible to move or think clearly.

He closes the distance between us, and my heart pounds.

There's no way he took the bait.

Is this really happening? Holy shit. Is he going to finally kiss me?

Wait. Did I shave this morning?

Oh, God. Why did I have to pick out my worst pair of period spanks today? It's not even that time of the month, but I've severely neglected the laundry, and considering I had no intention of even getting this close to Nick, I didn't bother to pack any of my good underwear. Worst decision of my life.

His head tilts down, that blueish-gray stare holding me hostage as my heart pounds with blazing intensity. "Every fucking day for six long years I've laid in my bed and imagined the way you would touch yourself. How you'd picture my tongue on that sweet little cunt as you rolled your fingers over your clit. How you'd picture my cock when you fucked yourself. Because you do, don't you? You still picture me because no one has ever made you come alive the way I did. Isn't that right, B?"

Oh, God. I'm screwed now, so why the hell do I find myself nodding, giving up my worst-kept secrets. "Yes," I breathe, hanging on his every word, completely captivated by the very sound of his tone. "Only ever you."

"That's what I thought," he rumbles, that deep tone thickening with the most intense desire, his lips hovering right by my ear. "Let me be clear, Blair. I will not fuck you until you're on your knees begging me to touch you again. Begging for me to take you back."

My hands start to shake, hunger pooling deep in my core, and just as I reach for him, he pulls away, stepping back and letting the cool air rush between us. "You're drunk, Blair. Go to bed."

I swallow hard, his rejection hitting me right where it hurts, but fuck, I deserve it more than I think I could ever really understand.

Nick doesn't hang around, not risking that lack of control he seems to have developed, and before I can even fully register that he's walked away, I hear the heavy thud of the front door closing behind him.

Asshole. What kind of man leaves his girl wanting like this? But I guess I'm not really his girl anymore.

Shit. Did he say he's thought about me touching myself every night for the past six years? Now I know I've had far too much to drink tonight, and getting my wires crossed where Nick is concerned is a favorite pastime of mine, but surely I didn't misunderstand him, right? Because no red-blooded man is just lying in bed with his hands casually hanging by his sides while thinking about a woman getting off.

I might have been thinking about him while going to town on myself, but he sure as hell has been thinking about me too, and that little bit of knowledge has a wicked grin stretching across my face.

Nick pictures me in bed. He curls his strong fingers around that thick cock and fucks himself while thinking about being with me.

Holy shit.

I don't know why this is coming as such a surprise. After all these years, despite everything that's been said and done over the past few days, I didn't expect him to still think of me that way. Sure, I thought there was a good possibility that he'd still love me. No one ever gets over their first love, but to think about me sexually . . . shit. It's a sobering thought, and I hate that I like it so much.

My thighs start to tremble. Rena was on to something about creating a naughty list.

Does he picture my face? My lips? The way my body would move as I ride him? Or does he picture me on my knees, taking me from behind with that strong hand firmly gripping my ass? Does he imagine how warm I would feel, how wet and needy I would be, or how my walls would squeeze around him, fitting so perfectly as though my body was made just for him?

Oh God, I'm definitely going to hell. Santa's not going to be the only one coming this Christmas.

My hand curls around the base of my vibrator, and as desperation pulses through me, I flop onto my bed, grabbing the blankets and hauling them up to my chin. More than ready to make a little Christmas magic of my own.

CHAPTER FIFTEEN
BLAIR

My head pounds with regret as I trudge through my house, groaning when I find the fire has fizzled out. A small sigh leaves my lips when I stop, my heart threatening to pound right out of my chest.

My feet pause, my brows furrowing, and I back up a step, turning to face the offending fireplace.

I cleaned that fireplace yesterday. There shouldn't be any charred remains. I go over the shady details of my night, trying to remember everything in chronological order. Nick unlocked the door, led me inside, and got a glass of water. He took me down to my room where we awkwardly found my trusty vibrator, and then after completely winding me up, he left.

Neither of us stopped to put the fire on, but it had to have been Nick after he walked out of my room because nothing else possibly makes sense. But I could have sworn he walked straight out. I heard the thud of the door when he left.

At least, I think it was the thud of the door, but in reality, it could have been any single door inside my home.

Ahh fuck.

This can't be happening. If he didn't walk straight out last night, that means he was still here when I went to town on myself with my vibrator. He would have heard every moan and sharp gasp I made. Oh, God! Even though the details are fuzzy, I definitely screamed his name in shameless desperation.

Oh no, no, no, no, no. This is not happening.

Humiliation sweeps through me. I already made enough of an ass of myself at the bar when I asked him to take me into the back of his pickup and have his wicked way with me. But damn, the way his eyes sparked to life as though I'd breathed pure oxygen right into his lungs for the first time in six years . . . Shit. What I wouldn't give to see that look in his eyes every day for the rest of my life.

Woah. Every day for the rest of my life? I shouldn't be thinking like this. I need to be focusing on the business I'm going to build very, very far away from here, not the life I'll never be able to have in Blushing. I walked away from those possibilities years ago, and until now, I thought I was content in that decision.

Being back here in Blushing is starting to screw with my head. Or maybe it's just whatever Oxley was pouring into my drinks last night.

Not wanting to freeze, I stride over to the charred remains of last night's fire and grab a few pieces of wood off the pile—a pile that's certainly fuller than it was yesterday. Strategically placing them into the fireplace, I quickly light it.

Pride drums through my chest. There are so many things I've had to learn about being a homeowner in an area like this, and lighting that fire has been one of the biggest learning curves of all. I've spent hours trying to get the hang of stacking the wood inside the fireplace correctly, but I'm getting there. Not going to lie though, if I ever had the opportunity to build my own house, I'd definitely be ordering one of those electric fireplaces. Or perhaps just installing central heat would be easiest.

With the fire now roaring and the house steadily getting warmer, I make my way into the kitchen, and just as I turn on the coffee machine, my open laptop comes to life with an incoming video call. I cringe at the sound, cursing myself for leaving the volume on max, but there's no denying the happiness I feel seeing Rena's name on the screen.

"Hey, Rena," I say, answering the call and swiveling the screen to face me so that I can keep making my coffee. "Bit early, don't you think?"

"Early? What the hell are you talking about? It's almost midday."

"What?" I grunt, whipping around to see the old clock on the wall. "Holy shit."

"Did you only just get up?"

"Yeah, I had a bit of a wild night at the bar," I mutter, willing my coffee mug to hurry up and fill itself. "Oxley was working the bar and after having Dwayne call to beg for me back, he made it his personal mission to get me as fucked up as possible."

"Oh shit."

I laugh, remembering it all too clearly. "Well, I wasn't exactly innocent in all of it. I had a shitty day and sat at his bar with every intention of wasting the night away, but then Sarah showed up, and she'd had a shitty day too, and then—"

"You finally crossed Nick off your naughty list?" Rena cuts me off, trying to finish my sentence for me as a cheesy, hopeful grin stretches across her face.

I groan and roll my eyes as the embarrassment of my night comes back full force. "As much as I wanted to cross him off the to-do list, I fully humiliated myself trying to do so, and that won't be happening. Besides, now that I don't have Oxley's potent concoction pulsing through my veins, the only thing I need to tick off my to-do list is a groveling apology. Not to mention, I'm pretty sure Nick was still in the house, lighting my fire, while I got myself off."

"Ummmm . . . what?" she laughs. "You've definitely missed parts of that story."

Embarrassment flushes my cheeks, and I pick up my full coffee mug, taking a long-awaited sip. "When Sarah and I got so drunk we could barely stand up, Oxley called Nick to come take our asses home, and then Nick walked me right into my bedroom to make sure I didn't kill myself on the way, and after an embarrassing encounter with my vibrator and me pretty much begging him to watch me use it, he stormed out saying he wasn't going to touch me until I was begging for him back and then . . ."

I cut myself off, the humiliation of last night suffocating my words. How the hell am I supposed to live this down?

"And then?" Rena prompts. "You can't get that far into a story and just stop mid-sentence. What happened?"

"Ugghhhhhh," I groan, not wanting to have to repeat it again. "He stepped into me and said some things that made me all . . . hmmmmm . . . and then he just walked away, leaving me all worked up, and when I heard the door close behind him, I—"

"Got to work," she booms, her laugh coming through my speakers in a high-pitched squeal.

"Like any other woman on the edge would do," I agree. "But this morning I realized the fire had been made, and I know for sure he didn't have time to light it before he forced me into my room, which only means he had to have done it after, right when I was—"

"Giiiiiirl," Rena laughs, enjoying this way too much. "That's so damn funny. I've heard you getting off before, and you are so not discreet about it. The whole foundation of the house would have rocked when you came."

My cheeks flush the brightest shade of red, and I bury my face into my hands. "What am I going to do?"

"Invite him to join in next time," she says, shrugging her shoulders as though it's that simple. "After all, you're still in love with him, right?"

I swallow hard and glance away, not having enough courage to face that reality this morning. "Did I show you my paint job?" I ask, more than happy to change the topic.

Rena rolls her eyes. "Subtle."

I smirk. "You wanna see it or not?"

"Show me."

Grabbing the laptop, I walk around the house, showing off all the work I've been doing before leading her into one of the spare rooms where I have piles of boxes. She talks with me for a while, helping me make the final decision on some of Nana and Pop's old things, whether they need to go into storage or be donated because I simply could not make the call myself.

Then on my way back to the dining table, she makes underhanded comments about my Christmas spirit throwing up in my living room. By the time I'm sitting back at my table, my stomach rumbles for lunch, and when Rena follows my train of thought and shifts, I realize the background is more than just familiar, she's in my apartment.

"Woah. Hold up," I say. "Is that my kitchen you're sitting in?"

"You're only just realizing now? We've been talking for over an hour."

"You know I can't function after a night of wild drinking. I'm lucky I'm even functioning today."

"Good point," she laughs before fixing me with a hard stare, worrying her bottom lip as though considering if she's even going to tell me what she's up to. "I was planning on saying that I was here to water your plants—"

"I don't have any plants."

"Yeah. The only downfall of my otherwise brilliant plan."

"Rena," I scold.

She lets out a heavy sigh. "Alright, fine. I'm packing up your apartment."

My eyes bug out of my head, and I gape at her like she just told me she spent the evening with her fist shoved up a gorilla's ass. "You're doing what?" I screech.

"You heard me. I'm getting a head start on the inevitable," she explains. "You might not know it yet because you're so hellbent on denying what everybody else can so clearly see, but Blushing is your home. It's where you're happiest and have all of the memories of your nana and pop."

"I get that, but New York is where I want to be. I put six years into building a career. I'm not just going to give it all up to go and be Nick's pretty little wife."

"No one is saying you need to give it all up. Hell, you'd be an idiot if you even considered throwing in the towel, but in this day and age, why do you need to be situated in New York to have everything you ever wanted? You have a great Wi-Fi connection over there in Blushing and have all the potential clients in the world. You've already proven yourself. You can be anywhere in the world and still make this business happen."

"You . . . you want me to run my new firm as an online business?"

"That's exactly what I'm saying," she tells me. "You have all the connections over here in New York and plenty of junior publicists who would kill to work under you, so use that to your advantage. Train them to take the in-person meetings while you thrive over there in Blushing. And who knows, maybe even open yourself up to love."

My gaze narrows, suddenly realizing this is so much bigger than just getting to remain in my hometown. She's doing this specifically to have me fall back into Nick's capable arms. She's doing this to give me the best of both worlds, and while I want it more than ever, I've already fucked up everything here in Blushing. Nick doesn't want me like he used to. I burned that bridge a long time ago.

"Look, I appreciate you wanting the very best for me, but I don't know. It's a lot to think about."

"No one is forcing you to make a decision right now. You need to focus on what you want from Blushing first, and then we'll see if this idea is even plausible, despite the fact that I know it is."

"It all means nothing if Nick doesn't want me."

"I mean, if you stopped screaming at him on the side of the road, perhaps you'd be able to figure it out," she says as I roll my eyes. Rena watches me for a moment, a seriousness coming over her. "You know, he'd be a fool to let you get away again. And as much as I would hate to see you leave New York and make new besties over there in Blushing, I'd never forgive myself if I didn't at least try to help you find your happiness."

"You really think I still have a chance with him?" I ask, knowing everything she said about having the new business being run online is completely plausible, otherwise, she never would have suggested it. Rena is renowned for doing her homework before making any moves. Unless it has anything to do with random yoga teachers or basketball players, then she's down to throw caution to the wind.

"I think you rolling back into town without warning has probably rocked his world, and he's terrified of getting hurt again."

"How could you possibly know that? Have you been talking to him?"

"No, but it's common sense, right? He's human, and it's clear from the way he keeps showing up for you, even though you're fighting him every step of the way, that he still loves you. Because if he didn't, he sure as hell wouldn't go out of his way to help you get home from a Christmas tree farm when literally anybody else could have offered you a ride home. Not to mention, he spent hours the next day trying to get your pop's truck out of a ditch knowing there would be nothing in return. No mind-blowing cock sucking session. No getting to bend you over and fuck you raw. He did it because he still loves you, because he wants you to be okay, and the thought of you going without or struggling sends him racing to your aid."

"Rena . . ."

"No, Blair. You have a real chance here. He's hurting, and if this is what you really want, then you need to put the effort in and make things right with him. You hurt him when you left, and that kind of heartbreak leaves scars."

"But my whole life is over there in New York."

"Your whole life was over there in Blushing once upon a time, too. But you figured out how to pack it all up and move across the country. If this is really what you want and you decide that you're ready to start the life you were always supposed to have, then we'll figure it out. I'm not going to leave you stranded. Hell, even if you need someone to meet with potential employees over here, you know I'm your girl."

"Shit, Rena."

"You're telling me."

I let out a heavy breath, hearing my phone beeping from down in my room. "This is a lot to think about."

"I know it is, but like I said, no one is rushing you to make a decision. You can still start up your business and get that underway while you figure out everything else. In the meantime, you owe it to yourself to at least explore things with Nick. And God knows he deserves a conversation from you—a real one, not some bullshit screaming match."

"I know."

"Alright, girl. Think on it."

"I will," I say. "And do me a favor. Stop packing my things. You're gonna mess it all up."

Rena rolls her eyes before purposefully grabbing the vase off my kitchen counter and putting it into the box beside her. "Whatcha gonna do about it?" she teases. "Love ya." And with that, the screen goes dark.

Letting out a heavy breath, I close the screen before getting up and making something to eat, only when my phone beeps again, I remember that a text had come through earlier. Striding out of the kitchen, I stop by the living room to put some more wood on the fire before having to scramble through my bedsheets in search of my phone. When I find it, the blood drains from my face.

A new text from a number I haven't received any communication from in six long years.

Nick.

I swallow hard, my heart racing as I open the text and quickly read over it.

Nick - Wow. Three times. I'm impressed. I was taking a wild shot in the dark guessing that you still thought about me when you came, but last night's performance was the perfect confirmation. Between you and me, you used to scream louder when it was me fucking you.

Holy. Shit.

CHAPTER SIXTEEN
NICK

A wicked grin spreads across my face remembering the text I sent Blair two days ago. I wasn't expecting a show as I knelt down in front of her fireplace to light the bastard up, but if she wanted to put on a performance, I was all too happy to take it all in.

Her groans. The way her bed creaked under her as she crept closer to her climax. The way she panted, gasping for air. But fuck, the self-control it took me not to burst down that hall and taste her when I heard my name on her lips almost took me out.

The first time, it brought me to my knees, and I couldn't even feel guilt for overhearing her like that. Hell, the moment has played on repeat in my head ever since. If only I could have snuck down the hall and watched her, seen the way her cheeks flushed, seen the way her back arched off the mattress, seen the way those beautiful thighs shook as she came. I've got one hell of an imagination, but it could never compare to the real thing.

Fuck.

I need to get a grip.

I'm not going to lie, after the first time she came, the fire was already roaring, but I couldn't bring myself to leave. My heart was probably pounding faster than hers. I sat on her nana's old couch and listened as she took herself to the edge, two and then three times. The sound was like music to my ears.

It was fucking glorious, the best Christmas present I could have asked for. Second to only one thing—finally being able to call her mine. But I'm a fucking fool for wanting that.

Shit. This makes me a fucking creep, doesn't it?

I snuck out before I could risk hearing her start for her fourth round, because if I had heard her again, I would have broken my vow to make her beg for it, but surely she didn't. She couldn't have possibly gone again . . . right? Hell, she always was a little firecracker, able to keep up with me perfectly. If she did go for a fourth, I wouldn't have been surprised. Hell, I should have stayed and applauded her efforts. After all, everyone deserves a party after achieving greatness.

After sending her that message, I watched as the three little dots appeared on the screen. They came and they went, and the process repeated for at least two hours, and all I could do was laugh. She definitely had no idea I was still in the house, but I'm guessing she pieced it together when she woke up and realized the fire was still burning.

She sure as fuck didn't expect me to call her out on it, though.

I've spent my morning at Hardin's Hardware picking up a few things to help Blair with the leaking laundry sink after getting stuck talking with Bessy at the grocery store. She made sure to remind me that I'd volunteered to be Blushing's most eligible bachelor for the Catch A Cowboy contest at the Christmas fair in a few days. Though, I don't know if volunteer is really the right word for it. It was more like being sucker punched into it by the horrifying visual of Blair catching another man.

Fuck. I wonder if she knows I'll be the cowboy she'll be trying to catch. The thought puts a wicked grin on my face. I hope it's just as much of a surprise to her as her arrival in Blushing was for me.

Pulling up outside her home, I grab the few tools I'll need and the replacement heater that I really should have picked up days ago before making my way to the door. She's not exactly expecting me today, but I have some free time, and if she tries to fix the sink herself, I'm only going to end up here trying to fix her fuckup anyway. At least that's what I keep telling myself. Truth be told, I've been dying to come back here since the second I left her panting in her bed.

Things are starting to shift. The anger in my chest has finally started to dissipate, and I'm seeing things more clearly. I think seeing the way she so easily fits back into life here in Blushing has put things into perspective, and I'm seeing my future flash before my eyes.

Blair has always been mine, and now the idea of her packing up and leaving again has me in a nervous sweat. I don't think I'm ready for her to leave quite so soon, and yet, here I am, showing up with bullshit excuses to help her with her renovations, which in reality, is only going to help her get out of here sooner.

God, I'm such a fucking idiot. If I were smart, I'd be coming up with reasons why this renovation needs to be extended. But at the end of the day, if she's going to remain in Blushing, I want it to be because she wants to be here with me, not because she has no other choice.

My knuckles rap against the old wooden door, and I take a step back, putting space between me and the door so that Blair doesn't have to barrel right into me the moment she opens it. Though come to think of it, maybe that wouldn't be such a tragedy. I'll take any chance I get to put my hands on her and feel that smooth skin beneath my palms.

The cheesy Christmas music stops, and I hear her moving around inside as she makes her way toward the door.

Fuck. Why is my heart racing like this?

Be cool, Nick. It's just Blair. It's not as though your whole future with her could slip away in the space of two seconds if you fuck this up. It's not as though this is the woman you've been desperately wanting to make your wife.

Shit.

As her footsteps reach the door and the handle turns, I hold my breath as she finally pulls it open.

There she is. So fucking gorgeous, and the way her cheeks are already flushed with paint smears across her forehead tells me she's been busy this morning.

Her eyes widen just a fraction, and I watch as she sucks in a breath. Hell, I wonder if her heart is racing just as fast as mine. "Oh, Nick," she breathes, clearing her throat as though there's suddenly something blocking it. "What are you doing here?"

A smirk pulls at the corner of my lips. "Your phone broken?"

Her brows furrow. "Huh?"

"I'm assuming you didn't get a new number."

Understanding dawns as her eyes widen again. Her jaw slackens, and I know without a single doubt that she's going to try and play this off, acting as though she doesn't know what I'm referring to. But let's be honest, it's not only been circling my head for the past two days, it's been circling hers too. "What are you—"

"Tsk. Tsk. I saw the read receipt, baby," I say, inching toward her, watching as her gaze lifts, always remaining on mine as though just as captivated by me as I am by her. "There's no denying that you got my message. The question is, why haven't you responded?"

Her cheeks flush a deeper shade of red, and it's the most beautiful thing I've ever seen. I step right into her, my arm circling her waist as I drag her back inside her home, kicking the door closed behind her as the sounds of that night play on repeat inside my head. I press her up against the closed door and she gasps, her hand pressed firmly against my chest. And damn it, those beautiful eyes are still locked on mine. All it would take is for her to look away, to break the connection, and I'd be able to pull myself back. But the thought of letting her go pains me now that I have her in my arms and her sweet scent pulses around me.

I lean into her, my lips grazing the soft skin of her neck, and as she tilts her head, opening up for me, I can't resist taking a small taste. My lips work their way up to the sensitive space just below her ear, and when she scrunches her fingers into the material of my shirt, holding on for dear life, I almost fucking lose it. Hell, at this point, I don't even know what happened to her replacement heater, all I know is that it's no longer in my hands.

A deep groan rumbles through my chest, and my arm tightens around her waist as though terrified to let go. "What is it, B?" I rumble as her chest heaves with heavy, panting breaths. "Why didn't you respond to my message? I know you're not ashamed that I heard you. I know you better than anyone in this town, remember? Better than anyone you could have met in New York, too. You liked that I heard you screaming my name because you know what it did to me. Don't forget that I have seen you at your most vulnerable, seen the way you look when you come, tasted you. So don't fucking lie to me, Blair, and don't even think about pulling the I was embarrassed bullshit."

My lips return to her throat, and I feel the way she swallows, her fingers bunching even tighter into my shirt. "At first I was humiliated, but just like you said, you've touched me in ways no other man ever could, and the second I remembered that, the humiliation faded away. But then I was just . . . disappointed."

I pull back enough to meet her stare, refusing to loosen my hold around her waist. "What are you talking about?"

"You didn't come to me, Nick." She lets out a heavy breath, and seeing the confusion in my eyes, she goes on. "You sat out here when you heard how desperate I was for you, and you didn't come to me. In another life, back before I walked away, you never would have let that happen. The second you knew that I needed you, you would have run to me. You would have torn down the fucking door just to get inside my room and give me what I needed. But the reality is, I don't get to have you like that anymore. You're not mine to hold on to. Not mine to touch or kiss—or love. And that's on me. I screwed us up, and I suppose that your message just put that into perspective."

My lips press into a hard line, and I drop my forehead to hers, needing this moment of peace with her more than I could have ever known. "No matter where you are in the world, Blair. No matter how much we've pushed each other away, if you need me, tell me. I will always come running."

My thumb slips beneath the material of her shirt, skimming over her bare skin. "Trust me, not storming down that fucking hallway and giving you exactly what you needed was killing me, but despite how much I wanted to, and despite the fact that you'd been drinking, I couldn't do that to you."

Her brows furrow. "What are you talking about? I wanted you to."

"Believe me, I fucking know that, and had you known I was sitting out here, I can imagine that you would have come out here and seduced me until I broke—and it would have fucking worked. But you're leaving, Blair. At the end of the day, getting to touch you like that again, getting to hold you and taste you is only going to make it that much harder when you inevitably walk away. I don't want just a piece of you for a fucking night, Blair. If I'm going to touch you again, it'll be because you're mine."

"I—" she starts, her fingers brushing down my arm, trailing all the way until her hand is curled around mine. "I'm sorry."

"You don't need to be sorry," I murmur, inhaling deeply before pulling away. "Just know that if we cross that line, and you leave . . . there's no coming back from it. It's going to hurt you just as much as it'll hurt me."

Blair nods, her tight grip on my shirt finally loosening, and I take the chance to step back before I cross the line I've drawn. "I ummm," she lets out a breath and shakes her head as if needing a second to find her bearings. "Why are you here? I don't remember mentioning to John that I needed anything today."

"I had time," I tell her. "Figured I'd fix that leak in the laundry."

"Oh, thanks, but I think I know what to do," she tells me. "It's on my list of things to do tomorrow."

"Just how many lists do you have?"

Her cheeks flush, and she glances away, her eyes sparkling like the star at the top of the most breathtaking Christmas tree. "I don't think you're prepared for that answer."

I scoff and make my way toward the laundry room, and she hurries after me. "Hey. I said I can do it," she whines at my back. "I appreciate you coming to help, but I've got it handled."

"Yep. You're an independent woman and all that crap. Got it."

"So . . . you're going to leave my laundry sink alone?"

"No," I say, striding into the laundry and putting my tools up on the counter. "I'm going to save us both the time and effort and fix it now so that I don't have to come back here tomorrow and shuffle around my schedule just to have to fix it after you've made it worse. But really, I appreciate your can-do attitude."

Blair groans. "You're impossible."

A grin pulls at my lips. "And you're my new assistant. Congratulations."

Blair rolls her eyes and lets out a resigned sigh before stepping deeper into the laundry room. "Fine," she grumbles. "What do you need?"

I open the cupboards beneath the laundry sink and point. "Get your fine ass under there and shut off the main. It's the—"

"I know what it is," she huffs before getting down on her hands and knees.

My grin widens. I really don't need the help. After all, I'm going to have to get down there anyway, but watching her do it is like the cherry on top of an insanely good ice cream sundae.

Blair gets back to her feet and fixes me with a hard stare, her arms crossed over her chest, unaware of the way the movement pushes her firm tits up. "Anything else, Nicholas?"

Hmmmm. The way she says my name like that has my cock twitching to life. Please, baby. Say it again. "Another turkey sub wouldn't go astray," I say with a cocky smirk as I grab the tools I'll need and step toward the leaking sink.

"You know, I wish I could but the bigwigs up in management just announced a new policy for the Wilder kitchen that men with little dick syndrome are no longer permitted to eat any form of sub within the dwelling due to their inability to fuck a woman into oblivion."

I slowly turn to meet her stare, and the second I do, she's locked in my hold. A smug smile flitters across her lips, and I can only imagine the mental high five she's giving herself right now. "You know damn well what I'm working with," I rumble, watching her smug grin falter before she visibly swallows. "And judging by the fact you're still screaming my name after six fucking years, nobody else's, that only proves that no one else has ever been able to fuck you like I do. Not even close."

She swallows again, and now I'm the one with a smug-as-fuck grin. Hook. Line. Sinker.

"There might have been someone," she argues, her voice hitching an octave higher, a clear sign she's talking shit. "Maybe two. Maybe even twenty."

I scoff as I reach for the tapware and start loosening them so I can figure out what's going wrong. "That's bullshit, and you know—" Water spurts up from the loosening tap, the pressure so great it shoots the tapware right up to the ceiling as water instantly drenches the laundry. "Ahhh fuck," I rush out as Blair's high-pitched screech almost deafens me.

"Turn it off. Turn it off!" she screams.

"That's what you were supposed to do," I say, dropping down beneath the sink and reaching for the main, quickly realizing that instead of turning it all the way off, Blair turned it in the opposite direction. I hurry to twist it all the way back, and the water quickly shuts off, but the damage has already been done.

I fall back to my ass, gaping up at the water coating the ceiling, and honestly, I'm fucking dumbfounded. I can't say that's ever happened before. Water drips all around me into the pools flooding the tiles and as my gaze falls to Blair, I can't help but smirk.

She's drenched, and not just like she's done a quick dash through the rain. She looks like a drowned rat. Long brunette locks stick to the side of her face as her top forms to her body like a second skin, her nipples hardening from the chill.

"What the fuck just happened?" she breathes, the corners of her lips pulling into an amused grin as she meets my stare.

"What do you think just happened?" I question. "Blair Wilder tried to help."

"What? Me? You're the one who unscrewed the tap."

I arch a brow. "Do you not recall when I asked you to turn off the main, and you were all like I know what that is, but apparently you don't because now the laundry is wetter than you were the other night."

Her cheeks flame, and she kicks at my foot. "Nick! Are you ever going to quit bringing that up?"

"Hell no. It was one of the best moments of my life, and I wasn't even involved."

Blair rolls her eyes and takes pity on me as she strides toward me and offers her hand to help me up, and just as I take it and she starts to pull me up, she slips on the water, a piercing squeal tearing from her throat. My heart lurches in my chest, and I throw my arm out, quickly catching her before she cracks her head on the tiles, and I settle her onto my lap, her knees on either side of my thighs.

Her eyes are wide, needing a minute to catch her breath as she simply gapes at me. "Holy fuck."

"Uh-huh," I agree.

Her chest heaves with heavy breaths as she rests her arms over my shoulders, and I can't resist sliding my hand around the back of her waist. It feels so fucking right having her in my arms like this. Like no time has passed at all.

Water trickles down her face, and I brush my fingers over her cheek, wiping it away before pushing the wet hair off her forehead. With each slight movement, she watches me in return, those bright blue eyes boring into mine.

God, she's so fucking beautiful.

Time seems to still, my heart thundering wildly in my chest, and before I know it, she's leaning into me as though some invisible force is pushing us together. Her hand captures the back of my neck, her nails gently digging into my skin, and in an instant, I lose all sense of control and pull her the rest of the way.

My lips crush down on hers, kissing her deeply, and she becomes liquid in my arms, melting into me as though she was always meant to be right here. It's fucking perfect, like everything is finally how it was always supposed to be, and when the shock wears off and her lips start to move with mine . . . fuck. It's pure bliss.

A soft moan slips through her lips, and I swallow the sound, devouring her kiss as though I've been starved for it, as though I couldn't possibly breathe without it.

This is my home.

Blair Wilder is my fucking home.

Our kiss deepens, and she tastes like freedom on my tongue, like the rest of my goddamn life. I lock my arm tighter around her waist, dragging her in closer until her body is flush with mine. It's the perfect intensity, exactly what I've craved since the moment I saw her through the living room window. But how the hell am I supposed to let her go now?

The thought is sobering, and I reluctantly begin to pull away, and as if sensing the same thing, she inches back. "I umm . . . I'm sorry," she breathes, her chest rising and falling with rapid movement, mirroring my own. "I shouldn't have . . . but it just . . . crap."

Blair releases her hands from around my neck and drags them down her face, but she doesn't try to peel herself away from me. All I can do is stare at her in stunned silence because I know exactly what I felt in that kiss.

Blair Wilder is still mine.

"It's barely even been two seconds since you said you didn't want to touch me because it's just going to complicate things and make them harder and there I go, kissing you like I didn't even try to hear what you were saying."

"Blair," I say as she begins to ramble. Her gaze shoots back to me, almost looking distressed by what we've just done. "I was the one who pulled you in. Now quit fucking overthinking it and get off me. You're sitting on my cock, and if you keep wriggling around, that kiss is going to be the last thing on your mind."

Her eyes widen just a fraction, and she hastily scrambles off me, getting back to her feet. I don't waste a second, getting up off the floor behind her, desperately needing to focus my attention on the sink and not the way her lips seem swollen from our kiss.

"I'll uhhh . . . grab some towels to dry up," she says, worrying her bottom lip. "Maybe a mop as well."

I nod and with that, she hurries out of the laundry as though she can't possibly get out of here fast enough. The moment she's out of sight, I am finally able to take a proper breath.

Reality starts sinking in, and I scold myself for making such a stupid fucking mistake. Kissing her was incredible, everything I've thought about since the day she walked away, but I wasn't kidding earlier. How am I supposed to watch her pack her bags and leave now? Especially knowing that after all this time, she's still mine?

There's one simple answer—I can't.

CHAPTER SEVENTEEN
BLAIR

It's the annual Blushing Christmas Fair, and I've never been so excited. Well, okay . . . maybe that's a lie. I could definitely think of a million other things I'd like to be doing, like creating time travel so I can go back to yesterday and kiss Nick in my soaking wet laundry room all over again, but the Christmas fair will have to do.

Bessy has gone all out this year.

The town center has been transformed into the most incredible winter wonderland. Santa has just come and gone to visit all the children of Blushing and ask what they want for Christmas. There are hard-working elves in incredible outfits that Bessy must have spent weeks working on. They've been busy handing out candy canes for all of the kids while discreetly handing Jello shots to the adults, making this more than my type of festival.

There's a Christmas kissing booth, a reindeer field with Santa's sleigh rides, an ornament arts and crafts station, and of course, Blushing's famous Christmas tree decorating competition where the men of Blushing fight it out for the quickest time to not only erect a Christmas tree, but decorate it completely with lights, tinsel, ribbon, and fifty assorted ornaments. Nana used to make Pop enter every year until he started complaining about his back being too sore. But between me and him, his back never bothered him a day in his life.

The fair opened at nine this morning and has been running all day, and now at almost five in the afternoon, most of the younger families have started to disperse, leaving the grownups to start shifting this family fair into a rowdy town party, but not before Bessy gets to put on her favorite event—the infamous Catch A Cowboy.

I've been dreading it since the moment I agreed to do it, but I stand by my decision to participate. There's no telling who Bessy has chosen for her most eligible bachelor this year, but when it comes down to it, all that's required of me is a little running around. I don't need to go showing off my track skills, not that I have any. I just need to make it look convincing enough to feign a decent interest in the game until some other woman gets to find the man of her dreams. Hell, all proceeds from today go to helping the soup kitchen to put on Christmas lunch, so it'll be worth it in the end.

There are roughly ten minutes until the main event is supposed to go down, so I make my way toward the dog park that's been transformed into a makeshift arena. Bessy is on the microphone, reminding our small town of the good that's coming from today's fair and urging them all to donate to the cause.

When I hear her begin to announce the Catch A Cowboy event, my gaze shifts around the arena. I see Sarah directly across from me with her husband and a few other familiar faces in the crowd, but there's one specific face I haven't seen all day. Oxley is about twenty feet to my left with his future husband, assuming the guy says yes to his proposal tomorrow night, and I take in the faces of the people around them. I see Nick's father, his younger brother, and even their family dog, Beau, but not Nick.

Maybe he didn't feel like celebrating the Christmas season this year. Totally plausible. Or perhaps he's just trying to avoid me after he made my knees shake with that kiss.

Goddamn. If I start thinking about it again, I'm screwed. It was everything and more.

The way his arm tightened around my waist and held me close to his chest as though he'd never let me go. The way his fingers gently caressed my cheek. The way his mouth fused to mine and devoured every doubt that I've ever had.

It felt right. It felt like for the first time in six years, I was exactly where I was supposed to be.

Maybe Rena was on to something about remaining here in Blushing. That kiss only proved that there's unfinished business between me and Nick. Well, that's a given. There's always been unfinished business between us, but even after lying dormant for so long, the embers are starting to sizzle beneath us, and now that he's finally in my life again,

I can't possibly walk away.

I owe it to myself to see this through, to see if we really do have a future worth fighting for. Hell, that's assuming Nick can find it within himself to forgive me for all the hurt I've caused him. He's been so angry with me since the moment I showed up here, and he has every right to feel that way, but beneath all of that anger, I know he still loves me. Though, that unease has been starting to fizzle out, and instead of having his walls up every time I see him, he's beginning to settle into it, even playing around and teasing just like we used to.

Bessy calls the volunteers to the arena, and I let out a heavy sigh before peeling off my winter coat to reveal the cute cowgirl outfit I managed to put together—a pair of Daisy Duke short-shorts, an old flannel button-down of Pop's tied at my waist, and to finish it off, my old cowboy boots. Hell, I even managed to shave my legs.

Let's face it, I'm going to freeze. There's no question about it, but it'll be fun while it lasts, and the second it's over, I'll be pulling my coat straight back on.

As other women enter the arena from the crowd in similar outfits, I do the same, striding out to take my position around the circle. There are ten of us, all evenly spaced around the big arena, and I don't miss the way they size each other up, taking this game far too seriously. A few girls look at me as though I'm their next meal, and panic flutters through my chest.

What the hell have I just gotten myself into? Am I about to be mauled by a bunch of thirsty women?

"A round of applause for our eager contestants," Bessy's voice comes over the speakers, and I scoff. Eager is a bit of a stretch.

The crowd cheers for their favorite event, getting into the zone for the most athletic race this town has ever seen, and when Oxley's voice sails over the crowd, my cheeks instantly flush. "HELL YEAH, B. WHOOP THESE BITCHES ASSES."

Holy shit.

More of the other girls start looking at me, suddenly wondering if I'm going to be a threat to their Christmas date with the town's most eligible bachelor.

Speaking of, I wonder who it will be. Knowing Bessy, she'll be hitting up every available guy in town, but in the past, she'd used this opportunity as some kind of match-making program. I remember back in my college days, three years running, the winners of this event ended up a real couple who are now married and settled down with babies.

No wonder these other girls look so competitive. They think this eligible bachelor could have the potential to be their future baby daddy.

"Alright, alright. Settle down," Bessy says as the crowd continues to go insane, getting into the spirit of the event. "Why don't we go ahead and introduce this year's most eligible cowboy?"

The crowd loses it, and I roll my eyes as Bessy is forced to wait. Not even the microphone could lift her voice over this noise. When the crowd finally begins to calm down, Bessy starts her usual over-the-top introduction. "Coming in at six-foot-four with a smoldering, deep blue stare and a grin that could knock any woman on her ass, please welcome to Blushing's favorite arena, Nicholas Carter Stone."

What. The. Effing. Fuck.

Nick strides into the arena wearing a pair of old jeans, well-worn chaps, and a pair of cowboy boots that make my mouth water, but it's the bare torso that really makes me squirm. I knew he'd gotten bigger since the last time I saw him. That was evident the minute I laid eyes on him, but the sharp ridges of his abs are insane, matched with the big, wide shoulders and defined pecs . . . fuck.

I'm a goner.

He struts through the arena, and judging by the way his chest seems to glisten in the fading sunlight, I can only assume that Bessy slathered him up in baby oil, and I bet the old bag enjoyed it too.

He's simply delicious.

And I'm clearly not the only one to notice.

The other girls around the arena eye him up like a bunch of wild animals. Their casual stares become hungry, and suddenly it's no longer just a race to get to him first, they're out for blood. They all want him and will stop at nothing to win their date with Blushing's most eligible bachelor.

My heart races as my game plan begins to shift. For some reason, I don't think I'll be hanging back and letting some other woman win this race anymore. Three seconds ago, I didn't give a shit who won. I was in it for the charity aspect, but now, I feel as though I'm fighting for what's always been mine, and this time, I'm not willing to lose.

I want that fucking date and a million more after it.

Nick casually glances around the arena as if putting on a show for the eager crowd and enticing his hungry suitors, but it only works me up more.

Over my dead body.

They're not having him.

Nick takes his position in the center of the arena and does a slow turn for the crowd, eating up the attention, but as he comes to a stop, he faces me front on, that wicked blue stare locked on mine. The corner of his lips twists into a smug grin, and I realize he's done this on purpose. He knew Bessy entered me into this damn competition, and the fucker didn't say a damn word.

That bastard. He knew exactly what he was doing, and his little plan is working because not only am I going to be running for him, I'm going to win.

"Come and get it," he mouths, holding his arms out wide, welcoming me in.

My jaw clenches, and my hands ball into fists at my side before risking a glance at my competitors. They look as though they've been training for this all year. How the hell am I supposed to beat out nine wild women who are all desperate for the one prize?

I think about the chances of me not winning, how Nick would be forced to take the winner out on a date, and how she would probably do anything within her power to seduce him. I see red.

My blood boils, pumping rapidly through my system.

I will not lose.

Nicholas Stone is mine.

"Alright, ladies. Are you ready?" Bessy asks over the microphone.

A few of the girls squeal out their enthusiasm, but I can't talk, I'm too focused. I'm in the fucking zone. The blonde directly to my right looks like my biggest threat, and I will take her down if I have to. But the brunette directly across from me, while she looks scrappy, I'm not willing to underestimate her. I bet she's fast.

If I know anything about Nicholas Stone, it's that he doesn't settle for a consolation prize. There's only one prize in his eyes, and I'm not about to make him wait any longer to claim what's always belonged to him.

"GET YOUR FUCKING MAN!" Oxley hollers from the side, leaning over the boards that separate the wild animals from the masses.

Nick grins, and I can't help but wonder if he appreciates Oxley's encouragement, or if he just likes the sound of his cousin calling him my man. Not gonna lie, I like it too. More than he will ever know.

"On your marks," Bessy's voice booms through the cheap speakers. "Get set . . ."

There's a long pause, letting the tension build throughout the arena, but if Bessy doesn't say go in the next two seconds, I'm going to break all the rules and make a run for it before any of these bitches can even blink.

The arena is silent, everybody waiting on bated breath, Nick's heavy stare locked on mine as a million silent messages pass between us.

"GO!"

The arena breaks into chaos as the lyrics to Big & Rich's Save A Horse (Ride A Cowboy) blast through Blushing. Nick takes off at the speed of light as the nine other women break into a wild sprint, and realizing I've already wasted a second, I kick into gear and throw myself into the race.

The girls run after Nick like he's their one shot at a Tiffany's fifty percent off discount, claws out and ready to cut a bitch where needed. Two of the girls crash into each other and get into a scrappy catfight, and as Nick barrels past me, heading the opposite direction and effortlessly avoiding the chaos, I take a moment to take it all in.

They're all coming for him from different directions, and suddenly, I don't care about winning the race. Nick is already mine, and neither of us needs to be the fastest in a ring to prove that. What I suddenly care about are these women thinking they can treat Nick like a piece of meat, and just like that, my target shifts.

I aim for the blonde who cuts across the arena heading straight for Nick, and as she flies toward me with her focus on Nick's toned back, my foot accidentally kicks out, and she goes down like a sack of potatoes, leaving only eight. Actually, make that six. The two in the catfight have taken themselves out.

A grin tears across my face, and as I glance back over my shoulder, looking for my next target, I catch Nick's stare, and judging by the way he's smirking at me with immense pride, he knows exactly what I'm doing.

I set my sights on the fiery redhead who seems to have a game plan of her own—catch him off guard. She slinks around the other side of the arena while the other five trail behind Nick. She plans to catch him head-on, hoping his attention is too focused on avoiding the women at his back.

She races toward him, mirroring his moves to always keep right in line with him, but that's not going to happen. Not on my watch.

I cut through the arena, running up the center toward her as my heart pounds, but no longer from the thrill of the race. I'm just exhausted. This is more running than I've ever had to do in New York.

I'm going to need a good drink after this, and it better be strong.

My pace slows, and I try to push myself a little faster. Realizing she might just beat me to him before I get my shot at taking her out. I feel like I'm racing at a snail's pace, but I ignore the way my lungs burn and push past it. Then just as she's about to cross in front of me, I throw myself forward, tumbling over my own feet and skidding along the dirtied snow of the arena putting me right into her path.

Nick is only a few paces to my other side, probably having watched my spectacular downfall. I cry out in pain as my hip takes the brunt of my fall, but I have no time to even think about it as the redhead is on me.

It happens all too fast. Her eyes are locked on Nick, and she reaches out her hand, ready to grab him, but not getting the chance to adjust herself, she's forced to try and leap over me, only her diamante studded cowgirl boots hit my shoulder and she tumbles over, face planting into the snow just as Nick sidesteps, quickly avoiding using her fallen body as a runway, leaving him no choice but to jump over me.

But he's not getting away with it that easily, and I'm sure as hell not about to let him get this close to me only to let him race away with a trail of girls heavy on his heels.

As he flies over my head, I throw my hand up, praying to the coordination Gods that I can somehow pull this off, and then in a moment of sheer luck, my fingers curl around the bottom of his boots and I grip on with everything I have.

His momentum has me all but flying up behind him, but as his ankle catches the whole weight of my body, he falls forward into the snow. I scream, barely able to hold on, and hoping like hell I haven't hurt him, but the second he's down, I scurry before any of these other girls can claim my victory.

I throw myself over his back, practically collapsing onto him as the exhaustion weighs heavily on my body. Hell, I can't even take a minute to enjoy the fact that I have my hands all over his half-naked body. "Ouch," he mutters from beneath me, his face covered in snow.

My forehead falls forward onto his back, my mouth squished against his skin as the rowdy crowd roars their approval. "I think I popped a tit."

"You don't have fake tits to pop," he reminds me as the other girls hover around, some collapsing to the ground as others brace their hands against their thighs and take big heaving breaths.

"I could have fake tits."

Nick groans and reaches for me, yanking me off his back and throwing me down into the freezing snow, but for once, it's welcomed. Then before I can even ask him what he's doing, his body is hovering over mine with my hand braced against his chest, his racing heart thumping heavily beneath my palm. "I committed every fucking curve of your body to memory, and these fucking tits are the same exact tits I've spent six years jerking off to, so don't try and tell me they're not real. I know your fucking body better than you do."

Heat burns between us, and my tongue rolls out over my bottom lip, not even caring if he wanted to fuck me right here in the snow in front of all these people. I've never been so worked up in my life. But before I get a chance to tell him just how much I want him, a rush of cold air hits my body as he pulls away from me and gets to his feet.

Barely a second passes when he reaches down and grabs my hand, hauling me up with him before inching my shorts down over my hip and checking for any damage from my fall. "You good?" he asks as Bessy booms through the speakers about finding Blushing's latest winner of our infamous Catch A Cowboy event.

"More than good," I murmur, bracing my hand on his shoulder as a grin tears across my face. "Amazing actually. You owe me a date."

Nick grins right back at me. "It seems I do."

CHAPTER EIGHTEEN
NICK

The canopy of fairy lights over Oxley and Ben's backyard sparkles like a million stars in the night sky, and it's the most beautiful thing I've ever seen—second to only one. Blair.

She stands across the yard, her gaze locked firmly on Oxley as he drops to his knee in front of all our family and friends on this wondrous Christmas Eve, taking Ben's hand and promising to love him for the rest of his life. All eyes are locked on them, watching in awe and happiness, but mine are locked on her.

There's a sadness in her eyes, a hollowness that mirrors the feeling deep inside my chest.

Oxley proposes to the love of his life, and it's clouded by the fact that I can't be with mine.

Last night at the fair was amazing. I knew Blair was going to go hard to prove something to herself, but in the end, she was proving something to the rest of the world. She's just not brave enough to say it out loud—that we still belong together after all of these years.

Our gathered family and friends cheer for the happy couple as Ben falls into Oxley's arms, but when all eyes are supposed to be on them, Blair shifts her gaze to mine, and I see in her eyes, exactly what's been messing with my head since the moment we got here—that should have always been us.

Blair presses her lips into a tight line, trying and failing to give me a small smile, but the heaviness is weighing her down. As her eyes pool with unshed tears, she slips through the crowd before making her way up the side of the property.

I try to give her space, but the second she disappears out of sight, my control slips, just as it always does with her, and I follow her out to the front of the property, finding her seated on the swinging love seat that used to belong to my mom. She has one foot beneath her while the other braces against the ground, gently swinging herself back and forth as she stares out into the night.

"You okay?" I murmur, leaning up against the frame of the old double porch swing.

She lets out a barely audible sigh, and the heaviness is even clearer. "I screwed everything up," she tells me. "I know you felt it back there, just like I did. That was supposed to be us. If I'd stayed, we would have had a whole life together, and I'm only now just realizing how much I lost. We could have had kids by now. Been married and built the home we always talked about, but I was selfish. I was thinking about the things I wanted and wasn't capable of seeing that there could have been other ways to get it. I should have stayed. You should have made me stay."

I shake my head. "You would have resented me and you know it."

Blair's gaze falls to the snow-covered grass, her shoulders slouched forward. "I don't know how to fix it," she admits, her voice getting choked up. "I broke us, and now . . . I don't know how to make the pain go away."

Fuck. It's one thing to miss what we had, but to be hurting like this . . . Her pain is my weakness, and if I could take the burden from her, just to make it a little easier to breathe, then I'd do it.

Inching toward her, I sit down in the space beside her, not hesitating when I reach out and wrap my arm around her slim shoulder, pulling her into my side. Blair immediately drops her head to my chest, snuggling into me as though I'm her only comfort. "I hate that you're still hurting, B."

"I've tried," she whispers. "I've dated and tried opening myself up to other people, but I always fell flat. I never allowed myself a chance to grieve what we had because I knew deep down that this was always my home. I wasn't willing to let go of it, and I . . . I miss you so damn much, Nick. I miss getting to call you every night and send you stupid texts. I miss when you would force me into your stupid truck and take me on ridiculous road trips. I miss everything, but mostly, I miss getting to be loved by you."

"Then come home," I tell her, enunciating every word and making sure she truly hears what I'm saying. "Come home to me."

"What?" she breathes, pushing up from my chest and meeting my stare. Her eyes are wide, filled with equal parts shock, hope, and fear. "I . . . but I ruined us. How could you ever want me to be here again? I thought you couldn't wait for me to leave."

I shake my head. "The thought of you packing up and walking out of my life again brings me to my fucking knees, Blair. How can you not see that? I'm fucking terrified of getting close to you because the moment you leave . . . fuck. I won't survive it again. I love you, Blair. I never fucking stopped, and for a long time, I wanted to hate you for how you tore us apart, but I never could."

She leans back in, her arm twisting around my neck, and I pull her onto my lap so she straddles me. "I'm sorry," she whispers again. "I hate that I hurt you, and I don't know how to make it right."

Reaching up, I take her face, holding her so damn close. "Come home to me," I tell her again, both of us knowing it's what's right, where we are both meant to be.

"I . . . I don't know," she says as a perfectly round tear falls from her eye and streaks down her rosy cheek. "I still have so much I want to do, and this business . . . My friend back in New York thinks I can launch it as an online firm, so staying here could be plausible, but then what? What happens if I come home? Do we just pick up where we left off?"

"Yes," I say without skipping a beat. "That's exactly what we do. Give us a fucking chance. I know you still love me, and it doesn't take a genius to figure out that this is what you want. Take the fucking leap,

Blair, and come home."

She searches my eyes, her hands falling to mine on her waist. "You really want this? You can forgive me?"

I lift my hand to her chin, gently holding her there and capturing her stare. "There's nothing to forgive," I tell her. "You left Blushing to chase your dreams, and that's not something I could ever hold against you. While it killed me having to let you go, I was also rooting for you, Blair. I wanted you to achieve everything you set out to do, and you better fucking believe that every time you got a promotion or stuck it to that dickhead boss of yours, I was cheering you on."

"You . . . wait. How do you know my boss was a dickhead?"

A small smile pulls at my lips, and for just a moment, I wonder if I should keep this to myself, but fuck it, she deserves to know. "I may or may not have had dinner with your nana every Monday night for six years straight, and she may or may not have broken every vow of loyalty between the two of you and told me everything that was happening in your life, right down to that loser Marc you were just dating. She wasn't very fond of him, but she loved talking about you just as much as I loved hearing it. Except for the Marc part. He sounded like a douchebag."

Her jaw drops, and she gapes at me as though barely able to believe a word I'm saying. "No. Nana wouldn't do that to me."

I scoff. "Damn right, she would. She thought it was hilarious, but only because she knew that one day, you were going to find your way back home. If she thought you'd moved on and were truly trying to find something real in New York, she would have respected your wishes, but at the end of the day, all she wanted was to share with the world how proud she was of you."

Blair's tears fall faster, and I pull her into my chest, loving the way she snuggles into me, just like she did when we were teenagers who thought they had everything figured out. "Thank you," she whispers as her fingers knot into my shirt. "I miss her."

"I know you do."

She lets out a heavy sigh, and I bring my fingers to her chin again, needing to see her face, needing to make sure that she's alright. The moment her chin lifts, those lips are suddenly on mine.

Electricity pulses between us, and I lock my arm firmer around her waist, holding her to me as her lips start to move on mine. I kiss her back, unable to resist the temptation, and within seconds, her body melts into mine.

A soft moan slips through her lips, and I hold her tighter, needing her closeness more than I need my next breath.

When she reluctantly pulls back, she drops her forehead to mine, her chest heaving. "Is now a good time to demand that date you owe me?"

A groan rumbles up my chest as my fingers dig into her hips, knowing it's not really a date she's asking for. She wants to take this further, she wants to feel the way we used to be when we were together, wants to feel the way I'd love her.

"You might not remember this as clearly as I do, you know, considering the amount of alcohol you consumed the other night," I say as my fingers fall to her thigh and slowly trail higher, teasing her with exactly what she wants. "But you might recall that I told you that I won't be touching you like that, not until you're on your knees, begging me to take you back."

She sits back on my lap, her hands falling down between us as she meets my heavy stare, and fuck, the way she looks at me with that intense hunger has me ready to take her right here on Oxley's porch. "I'm on my knees, Nick," she says, glancing down between us, and I mean, technically she's not wrong. She's straddled over me, her knees braced on the seat on either side of my thighs, but it's not exactly what I had in mind.

Her gaze lifts back to mine, almost knocking the breath right out of my lungs when she reaches up and hooks her hand behind my neck, leaning in close enough that her breath is nothing more than a slight tickle against my skin. "This is me begging," she whispers as the world fades around us. "I'm done trying to deny that this is right where I was always supposed to be. I want to come home to you. I want every part of me to belong to only you, and I want to build the life we were always supposed to have. Take me back, Nick. I need to belong to you again."

My heart pounds as I hold her gaze. "You want to come home?" I ask, barely able to believe it.

"I do," she says, her grip around the back of my neck tightening. "I've been in love with you since the day I first met you in high school, and I'm done trying to pretend as though being away from you like this hasn't been killing me. This right here, in your arms, this is where I want to spend every day of the rest of my life. I want to have a billion children who all share those same blueish-gray eyes of yours, and I want them to drive me insane. I want to build a home with you and fill it with memories. And... shit, Nick. Tell me you want this too because otherwise, I don't think I could—"

I take her face in my hands and crush my lips to hers, kissing her deeply as every ounce of resentment and anger fade from my body, leaving nothing but a brimming hope that we'll finally get to have everything we always deserved, and I'll finally get to love her the way I need.

"Fuck, I love you," I say between kisses.

"Nick," she pants.

"I know," I murmur as my hands scoop under her ass, and I lift us both off the porch swing. Her lips fuse back to mine, and instead of walking halfway down the street to find my truck in the mess of vehicles lining the street, I turn and stride through Oxley's front door. I don't have the patience to wait until I get her home. I need to have her now.

Making my way to the spare bedroom, I kick the door shut behind me before turning around and pressing Blair up against it. "Oh God," she groans as I break our kiss and drop my lips to her neck.

"God ain't got nothing to do with this," I warn her. "You scream for me, baby. I'm your fucking God now."

Her eyes roll as her fingers knot into my hair. She tilts her head back against the door as a low moan rumbles through her chest. "Fuck me, Nick," she pleads. "I need to feel you inside of me."

My fucking pleasure.

Blair's hands leave my hair and drop to my back, fisting the material of my shirt into her fingers and desperately tearing the shirt over my head. For just that second, I'm forced to pull back from her, but the feel of her bare hands on my body is worth it.

Her nails dig into my flesh, and I hope to God they leave marks. Not being able to wait another fucking second, I pull her away from the door, one hand gripped beneath her ass as the other dives between our bodies, searching for the button of her jeans.

Blair holds onto me, her arm locked firmly around my neck, barely managing to keep herself up, and if it weren't for the tight hold of her legs around my waist, she probably would have fallen by now. When I get to the edge of the bed, I throw her down onto the mattress. She gasps, and the sound is like music to my ears.

I gaze down at her, taking in the hunger in her eyes as she waits for me to make my move, but I'm so fucking desperate to have her that she won't be waiting long.

Grabbing her thighs, I pull her down the bed until her ass is barely hanging on, and I finish unbuttoning her jeans before yanking off her boots and tossing them somewhere over my shoulder. She pulls her shirt, trying to get it off while I dig my thumbs into the waistband of her jeans, finally able to peel them down her beautiful, toned thighs.

"Nick," she groans, the intense need in her tone making my cock twitch painfully, so fucking desperate for her, but despite my desperation, I'm going to take my time.

Once all of her clothes have been tossed aside, I simply stare at her, needing a moment to take her in. She's so fucking perfect, every curve of her full tits and hips, the slight definition of her toned abs, and the way she looks back at me with her bottom lip caught between her teeth. Fuck, I need to devour her.

I drop to my knees at the end of the bed, and Blair gasps, bracing herself on her elbows as she meets my stare. "Holy shit," she breathes, the sound barely audible.

Damn fucking straight.

Keeping my stare locked on hers, I take her thighs and hook them over my shoulders, opening her up to me, and she groans, dropping her head back. "Fuck, Nick," she moans, her chest heaving, but before her moans even get a chance to fade into the silence of the room, I lean in, closing my mouth over her needy clit.

Blair gasps, arching her back as she balances on one elbow, stretching her other arm through her legs and knotting her fingers into my hair. "Yes!" she cries, her body flinching as I flick my tongue over her clit.

I relentlessly work her body, remembering exactly how she likes it as I add my fingers to the mix, slowly pumping them inside of her, pushing in and out then curling them until she's shuddering beneath me.

"Oh, God. Nick," she pants. "Yes. Right there."

Her pussy contracts around my fingers, and I grin while I work, knowing just how close she is. I bring her right to the edge before holding her there as I suck and nip at her clit, my tongue giving its best fucking performance. When she can barely take it a second more, I give her what she needs, allowing her to detonate.

Blair comes hard on my fingers, her sweet cunt shattering around me as she cries out with my name on her lips. She tightens her legs around my head, but I don't stop working her clit until she finally comes down from her high.

When I pull back, her body relaxes, and she collapses onto the mattress, a lazy grin on her lips as she gazes down at me. "That . . . wow," she breathes. "You've been practicing."

I smirk. I haven't. Not really. There's not been anyone I've been remotely interested in having a relationship with since her. It's not like I've had a vow of celibacy. I've occasionally been with other women, but no one truly worth giving myself to. But now probably isn't the time to get into it.

Getting to my feet, I reach for my belt, loving the way she tracks my every movement.

Blair scooches up the bed, the anticipation burning between us, and as she bites down on that bottom lip again, I'd give anything to capture this moment forever. The intensity in her eyes and the hard peaks of her nipples. She's fucking gorgeous like this.

My gaze trails over her body, and while I already have it perfectly memorized, I've missed it. I can't wait to devour her, to claim every inch of her body, and remove the stain of any man who's touched her since she was with me last, and fuck, I won't stop until she doesn't even remember their names.

After undoing my jeans, I let them fall heavily to the ground, my cock springing free, and I instantly curl my hands around my thick shaft, slowly pumping up and down as I watch her suck in a breath, her chest rising with the breath, pushing her tits up as if begging me to touch her.

Blair's tongue darts out over her lips, and I stalk toward the edge of the bed, having thought about this moment a million times over. "You're mine, Blair."

She nods.

"Say it."

"Every last part of me, Nick," she declares. "I'm yours."

Kneeling on the edge of the bed, I lean in toward her, scooping my arm beneath her waist and hauling her higher so her head rests against the pillows. She hitches her knee up high, and I settle between her beautiful thighs, my cock resting against her hip.

My hand roams over her body, trailing from her shoulder down the curve of her breast and to her waist. "You have no fucking idea how desperately I've needed to touch you."

"Right back at ya," she whispers, her feathery soft touch grazing over my back as she lifts her chin just an inch. I quickly close the distance, dropping my lips to hers and kissing her deeply as my hand trails back up her waist before cupping her tit. My thumb brushes over her pebbled nipple, and she gasps into my mouth. She's always been so sensitive there.

Blair reaches between us, her small hand curling around the base of my cock, and my whole fucking body jerks. "Fuck," I grunt, breaking our kiss as I drop my forehead to hers.

Blair grins, knowing the power she holds over me, but we've always fought over who has the upper hand, and as I brush my fingers back down her body and past the apex of her thighs, a shiver trails over her body. Finding her entrance, I push two fingers inside of her, slowly pumping them in and out as she hooks her thigh higher over my hip, and in return, her grip tightens on my cock, and she starts moving up my length.

Reaching the top, she rolls her thumb over my sensitive tip, and I slam my lips back to hers, a low growl rumbling through my chest.

"Oh, God, Nick. I need you inside of me," she begs as I thrust my fingers deeper.

"Condom?"

"No," she breathes, her lips moving against mine. "Not with you."

Despite wishing I could live in this moment forever, I can't wait another fucking second, and before either of us get a chance to even breathe, my tip is at her entrance. I press my thumb over her clit, rolling slow, tight circles as I begin to push inside her. I've never taken a woman bare before, not even Blair, and the feel of her warmth as I push inside of her has my eyes rolling in my fucking head.

Nothing could ever compare to her.

I inch myself deeper until I bottom out, pausing there just a moment, both of us groaning with intense pleasure. "I need to move, B."

She nods, locking her arm around the back of my neck, those beautiful eyes locking onto mine. "Give me everything."

With that, I pull back, and just as she requested, I give her everything I've got. I fuck her with raw emotion, letting her feel how much I've craved her with every thrust, letting her know how deeply

I love her with every swipe of my lips over hers, letting her know that despite everything and the heartaches we've both had to work through, we're going to be stronger than ever.

My thumb keeps working her clit, and she throws her head back as she arches her back off the mattress, my balls tightening with every intense thrust.

"Oh, God. Don't stop," she cries out. "Please don't stop."

"I've got you," I promise her, pushing her right to the edge and feeling the way her warm cunt squeezes around my cock. I push her harder, taking her deeper, and with each new thrust, she contracts tighter.

She sucks in a breath, and I lock my arm tighter around her waist, holding her so fucking close that I don't know where her body begins and mine ends. I crush my lips to hers, desperate for a release, and then just as she lets out a loud, gasping groan, she detonates, coming hard on my cock.

I don't stop, rolling my thumb over her clit as her climax continues to build, her walls wildly convulsing around me, bringing on an overwhelming wave of pure satisfaction crashing through me. My body locks up, and as I thrust forward, burying my cock deep inside her convulsing pussy, I come hard, shooting hot streams of cum deep inside of her.

Blair finally starts to relax, and her body goes limp, barely able to hold herself up. "Holy shit," she pants, her heated gaze meeting mine as I hover over her, both of us unable to catch our breath. She gapes at me as though in shock. "We need to do that again. Like right fucking now."

A wicked grin stretches across my lips, and I drop a swift kiss to her lips. "My thoughts exactly," I tell her, tightening my grip around her waist and quickly rolling us until she's straddled over me, my cock still buried deep inside of her. "But this time, I want to watch you as you ride me, and when you come, you better scream my name, or we're going to do this all night, over and over and over again until you get it right."

Blair arches a brow. "And if I never get it right?"

"Then I hope you got plenty of sleep last night because you're gonna need the energy."

CHAPTER NINETEEN
BLAIR

The early morning sun skims through my bedroom window, and a soft smile spreads across my face as I reach out, feeling for Nick, only my smile falters, finding the other half of my bed as cold as the light dusting of snow building up on my windowsill.

No.

My heart shatters. I thought we were heading in the right direction. I thought we were going to work on this, but clearly I was fooled by everything that happened last night.

I thought we'd wake up together, that he'd yawn and pull me closer against his body just like he used to when we were younger. I thought we were going to be stronger than ever.

But he's gone. Not even a goodbye or a note left on the pillow.

Was last night some form of revenge sex? Did he reel me back in just to be the one to walk away and tear me to shreds? No, I refuse to believe it. That can't be it. I know Nick, he wouldn't purposefully try to hurt me, not in a million years, not even if I chose to walk away. It's not in his nature.

Maybe he's just not ready to jump so far in the deep end, maybe he wants to take it slow. If that's the case, I'll grin and bear it because having him in my life in any way is better than nothing at all. I've gone six years without him, and now that I know how much of a fool I've been, I can't ever go back. He's stuck with me, and if he doesn't like it, well tough shit. He can learn to deal with it. I'm not going anywhere.

I suppose we need to have a talk, one where we're not so overcome with raging emotions that we end up in bed before the conversation is over. Though, there's no denying that last night was incredible for so many different reasons.

The way he touched me. The way he dropped to his knees and made me come with his tongue.

Oh God.

Shivers sail down my spine, and suddenly this bed is way too hot.

Coming to Blushing, I knew I'd be waking up on Christmas morning alone. Hell, I've woken up alone for the past six Christmases, so why should this one be any different? But last night, when Nick decided to come home with me and hold me while I slept, I thought just this one time, it might have been different. He's probably had to run home to spend Christmas morning with his family, something I really shouldn't have any issues with, but there's no denying the small ache in my chest, an ache filled with loneliness.

Not wanting to dwell on it, I get out of bed and trudge down the hallway, and with every step I take, I feel Nick between my thighs. After having a quick shower and getting dressed, I head into the kitchen, and as I start making a coffee, I quickly check in with Rena to wish her a merry Christmas.

She drills me on Nick, and apparently I'm incapable of keeping my mouth shut because I tell her all about my night, but all too soon, she has to go to get on with her busy Christmas.

My gaze sails around the house. There's still so much that needs to be done, but I'm not feeling it today, so instead, I grab the keys to the truck and head out. If I don't get to have the kind of Christmas I was hoping for, then the least I can do is try my best to help others enjoy theirs.

I pull up outside the soup kitchen, and as I make my way through the door, I find Bessy madly slaving over the hot stove, and she immediately puts me to work, getting the attached hall ready to seat the many friendly faces that will come through here today. I keep busy, not having even a moment to myself, but it's exactly what I need.

It's creeping close to the start of lunch when everything finally starts to calm down and Bessy invites me to eat with her before the mad rush, and despite everything, I can't manage to numb the disappointment of not being able to spend my Christmas with Nick anymore. I politely decline and leave her to eat with the other volunteers and drive myself back home. Maybe I could break open a new bottle of wine and be the miserable loner Oxley jokingly accused me of being—a loser who drinks alone on Christmas day.

Just great. This must be a new low for me.

Taking the final turn onto my street, I notice a familiar red pickup parked out on the curb, and my brows furrow, watching as Nick stands at my door before giving up and turning back. Then hearing the sound of my truck putting down the street, he glances up, and the second his gaze locks with mine through the windshield, I realize we're about to have it out in the middle of the street.

Turning into my driveway, I don't even get a chance to cut the engine before he's at my door, pulling it wide. "Where the hell have you been?" he demands. "It's Christmas."

"Yeah," I mutter, reaching over to the passenger side and grabbing my handbag off the seat before jumping out and closing the door behind me. I storm toward the front door. "I'm well aware."

Nick catches my elbow and spins me back to face him, his gaze demanding every bit of my attention. "Where the hell were you? I've been driving around town all fucking morning searching for you. I thought you said you wanted to do this? I took your fucking word for it. So imagine my surprise when I get back here and you're nowhere to be found?"

My jaw drops, gaping at him as though he just told me he was capable of shoving his own fist up his ass only to have it wind its way up through his guts and out through his mouth again. "Your surprise?" I demand with a scoff. "What about my surprise when I woke up thinking it was going to be the first Christmas morning where I wouldn't have to wake up alone, and the moment I opened my eyes,

I found my bed empty. Do you have any idea what that felt like? I thought we were finally in a place where we could give ourselves a real chance at this, but apparently it was just about getting your dick wet for you. Or maybe it's some bullshit way to get revenge on me for hurting you the way I did. I doubt it. I like to think I know you better than that, but I suppose six years is a very long time. People change all the time."

"Are you fucking kidding me?" he questions, stepping into me and forcing me to inch back a step. "Do you even hear yourself? Hell, have you heard a fucking word I've said to you the whole time you've been back?"

"I sure as fuck heard it when you said you wanted me to know how long I was planning on staying so you could gauge how much damage I was going to cause before jetting off and leaving you to clean up my mess."

"That's not what I . . ." he pauses and cringes. "Okay. I might have said that, but that wasn't my finest hour, and we both know I was talking shit. I was trying to figure out how much time I had to make you realize this is your home."

"Nick—"

"Where were you?" he asks again.

I let out a heavy sigh, not sure why it even matters at this point. "I was volunteering at the soup kitchen."

He nods and inches closer again, taking my hand and pulling me against his chest. He brushes his fingers beneath my chin before lifting and forcing my gaze to his. "I left this morning to get you a decent coffee from the coffee house so you could wake up on Christmas with your favorite coffee and not have to drink that shit out of that ancient machine you have. The line was long. It seems everyone in Blushing had the same idea, but by the time I got back, you were gone," he says, nodding toward a take-out coffee cup that's been left on my porch. "I'm sorry you had to wake up alone on Christmas. I thought you'd sleep for longer considering the . . . workout I put you through last night, but I'm even more sorry that your first thought was to doubt my intentions for you because that means I haven't tried nearly hard enough to show you just how badly I want this with you."

"Shit," I murmur, pushing up onto my tippy toes and throwing my arms around his neck. "No, I'm sorry," I tell him as a soft flurry of snow begins to dust the ground. "There you were doing this amazing, thoughtful thing for me, and I took off instead of having faith that you'd come through for me. I ruined our first Christmas together."

He shakes his head. "I should have left a note in case you woke up. That's on me. I made a bad call, but for the record, my coffee was outstanding. You would have loved it."

I groan, and he laughs, pressing a kiss to my forehead. "It's barely even lunchtime," he tells me. "This Christmas hasn't been ruined yet. There's still time to salvage the rest of our day. Besides, I plan on spending a million more years at your side, so we still have plenty of chances to fuck up Christmas, but today won't be that day. You're coming home with me."

My brows furrow. "To your place?" I ask as it occurs to me that I actually have no idea where he lives, which street, or even which part of town.

He watches me far too carefully. "Why do you say that like you're expecting me to chain you in my basement once I get you there?"

"I just . . . I don't know. I suppose that when I thought of you over the years, I always pictured you the way you were when I left, like you were frozen in time. And back then, you were still living at your parents' house. It's hard to imagine you having this whole life that I've never known about."

"You mean to tell me that this whole time you've been assuming I was still living at home in that small bedroom with my Megan Fox poster on the wall?"

I shrug. "I mean, no. I guess part of me assumed you might have eventually bought a home, but I could never picture what it would have looked like. I could only ever picture the home we always talked about building together, but obviously that wasn't going to happen, so I was left only with what I already knew."

A small smile pulls at the corner of his lips. "Come on. Get your ass in my truck. Apparently I have a lot to show you."

My brows furrow, but he doesn't give me another chance to question him before he leads me to his truck, his hand resting on my lower back. Then being the perfect gentleman, he opens the door and helps me in. "By the way," he says, standing in the open door, my hand pausing on the seatbelt as I meet his blue-gray eyes. "Merry Christmas."

Warmth spreads through my chest, and I lean into him, capturing his lips in mine in a swift, yet lingering kiss. "Merry Christmas, Nick," I murmur, my lips gently moving against his.

Nick holds my stare for a moment longer, and while I can tell there's something he needs to say, he pulls back and closes the door before making his way around. He gets in and starts the engine, the old truck rumbling to life. "It's not going to break down in the middle of town, is it?" I tease as he hits the gas.

"Those are fightin' words, baby," he says, his eyes sparkling with silent laughter.

A wicked grin cuts across my face, and as Nick makes his way to the outskirts of town, I pay close attention to where he's going. There's not much out here. Larger rural properties with big homes, their neighbor sometimes miles away. "Where are we going?" I ask, watching as the beautifully landscaped properties pass us by.

"Patience never was one of your strong qualities, was it?"

I scoff. "And you have the nerve to accuse me of using fighting words."

Nick laughs, and as he reaches across the center console and takes my hand, butterflies swarm through the pit of my stomach. "Only a few more minutes," he says, taking pity on me. "We're nearly there."

Excitement brims in my chest, and my knee bounces with nervous anticipation right up until he starts to slow, pulling off toward a dirt road. He drives along it, passing through thick forest, and then suddenly the trees thin into a clearing, bringing us to a fancy iron gate with the name STONE worked into the intricate design. "Holy fuck," I grunt, gaping at the massive gate.

"Not bad, huh?" Nick says with pride.

He creeps toward the gate, and it's then I realize that the dirt road has turned into a pristine one that looks as though it was handcrafted by the angels of heaven. Nick drives up to a keypad and enters a code, and as the gates start to swing open, I'm met with acres of what I can only assume is beautifully landscaped property covered in a thick layer of snow. The driveway is clear though, and I can only assume that Nick either spends every spare minute of his life shoveling it or that he dropped a bomb on underground heating.

Nick drives through the gates and onto the property, and it doesn't go unnoticed that he leaves the gates open behind him, but as he drives around the bend and the house comes into view, the gate is the last thing on my mind.

This home is everything I've ever wanted to build for myself, a vision plucked right out of my brain, and I gape at it in shock. It's a gorgeous two-story farmhouse with a wrap-around porch, the perfect home to raise a family. There's space to run and play, room for a barn and every animal under the sun.

"It's beautiful," I say, my voice cracking as I gape at the spectacular home. "This is really yours?"

"Mmhmm," he says, pulling to a stop right out front. "Took a little over four years to build, but it was worth it."

My eyes widen, and I turn my stare on Nick. "You built this?"

"Sure did," he says. "Every last bit of it was all me. Some nights I worked until my fingers bled, but I wouldn't change it for anything."

"Holy shit," I breathe, barely able to comprehend just how big of a job that would have been. "That's incredible, Nick. I . . . I don't even know what to say. How the hell could Nana just let something like this slip?"

Nick laughs. "Come on. I have just enough time to give you the grand tour before my family should be showing up for lunch."

"Your family?"

"Every last one of them."

Fuck.

I am so not prepared to face them. It's one thing having to earn Nick's forgiveness for breaking his heart, but his family has always been a tight-knit group. Breaking Nick's heart meant I broke theirs too, and just like Nick, they're not afraid to let me know. Hell, I'm sure they'll have plenty to say about the idea of Nick and me getting back together.

Jumping out of Nick's old truck, I meet him around the front, and he takes my hand before leading me to the front door. There are four small steps that lead up to the beautiful wrap-around porch, and the second my feet land on the hardwood, butterflies begin soaring through my stomach.

Nick reaches for the door handle, and it doesn't go unnoticed that it's been left unlocked, but I suppose when you live all the way out here on the outskirts of a crime-free small town with a big-ass gate keeping people out, locking up isn't quite as necessary as it would be elsewhere.

He welcomes me into his home, and my jaw instantly drops. It's absolutely stunning—a definite bachelor pad that could probably use a woman's touch, but the home he's built is incredible. It's an open plan, and from the front door I see the massive kitchen, dining, and living areas. As I take it all in, my gaze stops on the one thing that has no place in such a beautiful home.

"What kind of pathetic Christmas tree is that?" I ask, taking in what looks to be some kind of bushy stick with a single line of tinsel tossed over it.

Nick scoffs. "It's better than your burned one."

"That twig doesn't even come close to my masterpiece."

Nick rolls his eyes and empties his pockets out onto the small entryway table before stepping into me and crowding my space. "You've got no fucking idea how long I've wanted to have you inside my home," he murmurs as his hands come to the front of my coat and slowly open it before letting the heavy material fall down my arms. Without moving even an inch away from me, he reaches out and hangs my coat on the rack by the front door before leaning in and closing the gap between us. His fingers caress the side of my face before his lips are on mine.

It's a swift, passionate kiss, and all too soon, he pulls away, his hand falling into mine. "Let me show you around."

Nick pulls me along, showing me every last feature of the house and telling me everything about how he came to design each part, what inspired him, and anything worth noting along the way. By the time we've been around the whole house and we're back in the impressive kitchen, I'm absolutely blown away.

"It kept me busy," he says as I lean against the counter. "Kept my mind occupied so I wasn't always thinking about boarding a flight to New York and bringing your stubborn ass home."

A smile lingers on my lips as I push away from the counter and move into his arms. "I absolutely love it," I tell him, suddenly able to fill in all the blanks from the past six years and picture the life he's had without me.

Nick adjusts himself so that he faces me, his arm locking around my back as his blue gaze settles onto mine. "I built it for us, Blair," he says. "It was supposed to be your graduation present after college. I was waiting for the sale to go through when you told me you were leaving."

Shock bursts through my chest, and within seconds, I'm filled with a heavy guilt that rests on my shoulders, and I drop my forehead against his chest. "I'm sorry."

"Don't be sorry," he tells me, his hand roaming over my back. "It is what it is, and what matters is that you're here now. Despite the fact that you've never been here before, this has always been your home. I built it for us, for the life we always talked about, knowing that one day, you'd come back to me. Every inch of this place was designed with you in mind. The bedroom with the massive walk-in closet. You know damn well I don't have enough clothes to fill that, and the bathtub. I don't take baths, but I know you always loved them."

My gaze lifts, meeting his. "You built this for us?" I whisper, a lump forming in my throat.

"I did," he confirms. "When I asked you to come home to me, I wasn't just asking you to move back to Blushing. I want you here with me. I want us to finally start our lives together. I love you, Blair, and that's never going to change. Seeing your face for the first time after so long last week was like finally seeing the sun after living in pure darkness. You breathed life back into me, and I'm not about to let you go again."

My heart swells as my eyes fill with tears, and I realize just how wrong I was to doubt his intentions this morning. Nick reaches up, brushing the tears off my cheeks as my gaze lingers on his. "Are you asking me to move in with you?"

"I am."

"I thought you just wanted to pick up where we left off," I muse. "But moving in? That's . . . that's not just picking up where we left off, it's taking leaps and bounds."

"And yet you know it feels right," he tells me. "So, what do you say? You can take over the home office to build your new business by day and we can work on the renovations on your nana's place by night, but at the end of the day, I want you crawling into that big fucking lonely bed down the hall."

"Are you really sure?" I ask, my heart thundering a million miles an hour. "You know I'm not the best to live with. I'm a slob, and I leave half-eaten cartons of ice cream out on the counter to melt, and even then, I still eat it."

Nick laughs, taking my waist and lifting me onto the counter before stepping between my legs, his lips brushing over mine. "I know all of this about you, and despite your disgusting habits, I still want you. Every fucking part of you."

A smile pulls at my lips, and just as I go to tell him that nothing could ever make me happier, the front door flies open with all the familiar faces of Nick's family. His dad, his brother, Oxley and his new fiance, and even the family dog Beau.

"Blair!" Nick's brother, Nate, storms through first, shoving Nick out of the way and grabbing me off the counter. He spins around, and I squeal, certain I'm about to die. "'Bout time you came to your senses."

"Get your hands off my fucking girl," Nick grunts at his brother as the dog races up to me and sniffs at my legs, desperate for attention, and judging by the way he jumps up on me, he remembers exactly who I am.

Nate puts me down, and I instantly bury my fingers into Beau's thick fur, scratching his head simply for existing in my world. "You owe me fifty bucks," Nate says to his father, earning an eye roll out of Nick before turning that familiar gaze back on me. "That was quite the show you put on at the Christmas fair."

"They were looking at him like he was a piece of meat."

"Let me guess," Oxley teases, striding through to the kitchen. "You're the only one who's allowed to do that?"

"Damn right," Nick murmurs, stepping back into me and burying his face into the curve of my neck, his lips softly brushing my skin with the sweetest kiss.

"Alright, alright," Nick's father mutters. "It's great to see you Blair, but put some distance between the two of you. Nobody is making babies on my watch. We have a Christmas lunch to make. Now, you know the Stone family rules, Blair. If I can see you, I'm putting you to work."

I laugh, pulling out of Nick's arms and loving the way his hand discreetly falls, grabbing my ass. "Where do you need me?"

With that, Oxley grabs a huge raw turkey and drops it onto the kitchen counter before giving it a good spanking. "Ever fisted a turkey?" he asks, his lips kicking up into a wicked grin. And just like that, I'm welcomed straight back into the Stone family as though I was never gone.

CHAPTER TWENTY
BLAIR

Who would have known that leaving Christmas lunch up to a bunch of men meant that lunch was actually going to be dinner, and for the most part, it was burned, but I wouldn't have it any other way. Today has been an incredible day, and as I stand with Nick, watching as his family drives away down the long, winding driveway, I finally feel at peace, knowing we're doing the right thing.

His hand lingers on my lower back, and that one gesture is filled with so much love and adoration, I don't know how I found the strength to walk away from him in the first place. I fold into him, needing to feel the rush of being in his strong arms.

"That was amazing," I tell him. "I thought they were going to hate me for breaking your heart and being away so long, but they treated me like part of the family."

"Because that's exactly what you've always been," he tells me. "Plus, they know Mom would haunt their asses if they were anything less than perfect."

A fond smile spreads across my lips as I pull back just enough to meet his gaze. "It was weird seeing them all without her," I tell him, though I know he feels it. "I'm sorry she's gone. I wish I could have been here for you. I can't imagine how hard that must have been for you. I know you were close."

Nick nods. "Just having you here now helps," he says. "Some days are harder than others."

"Just like with Nana."

"Exactly."

Nick leads me back inside, and with the house all cleaned up after such a disastrous cooking experience, we're finally free to relax. We make our way into the living room, and Nick turns off the lights, leaving nothing but the expansive view out of the floor-to-ceiling windows of the huge property and the crackling fireplace that sends warmth through my cold fingers.

The moonlight is just enough to cast a glow across the property, and it's absolutely breathtaking. "I'm an idiot for walking away from all of this," I whisper as we snuggle on his large couch.

"I know I should give the typical response and tell you that you're not an idiot. That you were chasing your dreams and that I'm so unbelievably proud of you for taking that risk and doing what so many others could only dream of. Buuuuut yeah. You're a fucking idiot."

"Nick!" I laugh, swatting at his wide chest. "You're such an ass."

He smirks and reaches for me, pulling me onto his lap. "I'm an ass who's still waiting for an answer," he says. "Don't act like I haven't noticed you left me hanging."

"Oooh, I don't know," I tease. "I'd love to live here. Apparently the dude who built it was so crazy about me, he practically pulled the design right out of my brain. But it seems the property comes with an overbearing assface who's going to be sleeping in the same bed, and I just don't know if I should be putting myself through that kind of torture."

Nick flips us before I even get a chance to suck in a gasp, and suddenly my back is against the soft backrest of the couch with Nick's strong thighs beneath me, forcing my legs wide. He bears down against me. "If you're not careful, this overbearing assface is going to torture you all night long."

"Mmmm, I wouldn't call that torture," I groan, my hand slipping beneath the fabric of his shirt and feeling the toned, warm skin beneath. "I'd call that making up for lost time."

He crushes his lips to mine, and the tension between us explodes, replaced by nothing but pure, animalistic hunger and need. He grabs my blouse, tearing through the buttons in his desperation for my body, and I hear the little buttons scatter across the hardwood floor, but nothing else matters but feeling him push into me, stretching me wide.

"Oh God," I groan as he drops his lips to my neck.

"I'm not fucking you until you tell me exactly what I want to hear," he growls, and despite his comment, his hands don't stop flying over my body, removing the pieces of my clothing as I do the same, madly fisting his shirt and yanking it over his head.

"You already know my answer," I pant as he reaches for the front of my pants, furiously trying to yank them down, only with the way I'm seated over his thighs, it'll be impossible. "You knew my answer before you even asked me."

"Blair," he groans, sounding pained. "I need to hear it."

I smile against his lips as his arm locks around my waist, lifting me just enough to get my pants down past my hips and down my legs. Then as I'm completely bare for him, he settles me back onto those strong thighs. "Of course I want to move in with you, Nicholas Stone. I want it so bad. I've already started working out how I'm going to organize my clothes in that massive walk-in closet."

A deep growl rumbles through his chest as he expertly works his belt buckle with one hand and releases his fly before freeing that thick, veiny cock. I reach down between us, curling my fingers around his base, and the sound that follows almost sends me to the darkest pits of hell. Anything that feels this good should be a crime.

I pump my fist up and down, but neither of us has the patience to draw this out. "Nick. Please."

Before the words are even finished slipping through my lips, he's already there, inching my hips higher as his other hand curls around mine, guiding his tip to my entrance. He pushes inside of me, barely just the tip, and already, I feel myself starting to stretch around him. He's so fucking big. I could barely close my fingers around him.

Nick pushes deep, and with every inch he claims, my groan of pure pleasure gets louder until he bottoms out. "Fuck, baby," he grits through a clenched jaw. "So fucking sweet for me."

"Only for you," I respond, panting heavily.

He rocks his hip, his cock pulling back before slamming forward again, and I throw my head back in pure bliss. "YES!" I cry, needing him to take me right there over and over and over again. "More."

Nick's fingers dig into my hips as my back arches off the soft couch cushion, and my head tips all the way back. He closes his lips over my pert nipple, his tongue flicking over the sensitive bud and sending an electric shot pulsing right through to my core, and it's everything.

My eyes roll in the back of my head, and I can't help but reach down between us and roll my fingers over my clit. "That's right, baby. Show me how you touch yourself."

I give him exactly what he wants, and as he fucks me within an inch of my life, my walls start to shake. It's too much, so damn good. I need it all, everything he's got.

"OH, God, Nick. Yes. So good," I groan as my fingers work in tighter circles, my chest heaving as I struggle to catch my breath. "Don't stop."

He fucks me like the king he is, and I'm his queen, and damn it, I've never felt such intensity or a deep connection, not even before I left for New York, and I know without a doubt that this right here is my forever.

Hooking my arm around his neck, he lifts his gaze to mine, those deep, loving eyes filled with all the love in the world. "Nick," I whisper, my lips brushing over his. "You're everything I've ever needed."

I feel his smile on his lips as his big hand curls around the back of my neck, and despite the way he fucks me with such urgency, a breathtaking softness appears in his blue-gray eyes. "I love you too, Blair," he tells me, every word spoken directly to my soul. "I'll never let you go again."

His lips move over mine, and I kiss him back, his taste intoxicating as my whole body melts into his. He takes my knee and hitches it up high, adjusting the angle as he thrusts into me, and my eyes immediately flutter. "Fuck, Nick. I'm gonna come."

"Let me feel it," he growls, the soft vibrations in his chest rumbling against mine. "Let me feel how that pretty cunt squeezes me, baby. Come undone for me."

Oh, God. His words are like the kiss of death, holding every bit of power over me, and as he thrusts into me one more time and my fingers roll over my clit, I detonate, my high blasting through me like a beautiful explosion.

My walls clamp down around him, and he curses under his breath, his whole body jolting, and as my pussy starts to convulse, he comes hard, shooting hot spurts of cum deep inside of me. "NICK!" I cry out, desperately panting as my nails dig into his strong shoulder, the intensity of my orgasm climbing to new heights.

He buries his forehead against my shoulder as a low groan rumbles through his chest. "Fuck, B," he breathes, his arm loosening around my waist.

Nick doesn't stop moving, drawing out every last second of my orgasm until I can finally start to relax, both of us coming down from our intense high. He adjusts us on the couch, laying down against the cushions and bringing me down with him, somehow managing not to pull himself free in the process.

My body collapses heavily against his, and in the past we've been able to get right back into action, going for round two or three, but that was so intense that I need a few minutes before I can even lift my head to meet his lovestruck gaze.

His fingers roam over my back, slowly trailing up and down my spine as goosebumps spread across my skin. "I could stay right here forever," I whisper into the night, my gaze lingering on the fireplace with the soft glow of moonlight filtering in through the large window.

"That's all I'll ever ask."

"Just an eternity of having to put up with your bossy ass, huh?"

Nick grins, his hand shifting down to my ass and squeezing tight. "Don't act like it doesn't turn you on. I see the way your thighs clench when we get into it. You crave the back and forth. It gets you all hot and bothered, and your cheeks start to flush, just like they are now."

"Oh yeah?" I challenge. "And when I do get all hot and bothered, what are you gonna do about it?"

"Baby, I don't think you're ready to know what I plan to do about it."

A wicked grin stretches across my lips, and I push up against his chest to look him right in the eye. "Try me."

His arm locks around my waist, and before I even know what's happening, we're halfway down the hall, his eyes flashing with the hunger of a new challenge. And with that, Nicholas Stone spends the rest of our night proving to me over and over just how good it really gets, not daring to stop until my throat is raw from screaming his name.

EPILOGUE
NICK
FIVE MONTHS LATER

My feet drag as I walk out of Hardin's Hardware after checking on John, and just as I reach for the door handle of my old red pickup, my phone sounds with a notification from my home security app, letting me know there's movement on the property.

My brows furrow, and I pull my phone out of my pocket, hoping like fuck that everything is okay. Blair works from home with her new business that's taking off like a fucking rocket, and she's generally so busy during the day that she only turns off the internal alarms, leaving the outdoor motion sensor alarms on. Not that we've ever needed it. The only people who ever come out to the property are my family and Sarah. Apart from last month when Blair flew her best friend Rena out to spend the week with us so she could share the news of her pregnancy. She's three months along, and we couldn't be happier.

Dropping down into my truck, I wait for the live footage and groan a moment later, finding Blair standing out on the front lawn, her hands up in front of her as if trying not to scare something away. Her back is to the camera, and despite her body half concealing the animal in front of her, there's no mistaking the giant fucking calf.

She slowly approaches the scared animal before offering it the back of her hand, allowing it a moment to get her scent. "Where's your mommy, sweet baby?" she coos to the miniature cow, her voice barely coming through the system. "Are you lost?"

Blair inches closer, and the calf immediately steps into her, rubbing its head against her, and I don't miss the way she subtly turns so the calf doesn't hit our baby growing inside her womb. It snuggles up to her, and as Blair's shoulders sag, I groan, realizing I just became a cow father.

"Are you hungry?" she murmurs, her hands rubbing all over the calf, giving it a good scratch. "Come on, my sweet little angel. Let me get you fed."

Blair turns and starts making her way back to the house, and the little calf follows her instinctively as though she just became its adoptive mother. I watch Blair a moment longer, expecting her to leave the calf in front of the house as she runs in to figure out how the hell to feed the poor animal, but my jaw slackens watching as a calculated smirk stretches across her lips and she ushers the calf up the four steps leading onto the porch.

No. No fucking way. She's not about to let that thing into our house.

"Please, baby. No," I groan, knowing damn well she can't hear me.

It only takes a minute or so for the calf to figure out the stairs, and then it's game over for me. Blair opens the front door and the little brown calf strides right through as though it owns the place.

It takes me a minute to switch the security camera, having to exit out of the external feed and to the internal one before having to figure out which room she's just waltzed a wild cow into.

Having Blair back in my life has been nothing short of an adventure, though there's no denying that we're constantly butting heads. It's part of the reason why I love her so much. We've been this way since we first got together in high school, but one thing is for sure, I will never attempt to renovate a house with Blair Wilder ever again.

When her nana's home sold a few weeks ago, it was the greatest news of my life. Don't get me wrong, I get that it was a bittersweet moment for Blair and she was an emotional wreck, feeling as though she was having to say goodbye to all of the fond memories she had growing up in that home. But fuck, I'm glad to see it gone.

The home went to a young couple with two little kids who had only just moved into town, a family who now gets to start their own journey and make new adventures every day, but shit, Blair and I fought every time we stepped foot into that house together. She had her YouTube tutorials on how to hang a door while I had the actual know-how, but that girl is nothing if not stubborn. When she puts her mind to something, everybody else better watch the fuck out.

I got steamrolled out of that house so damn quickly, I ended up sneaking back in during the day while she was working to fix everything she'd worked on the night before. Not going to lie though, by the end, she was really starting to get the hang of it.

Finding Blair in the kitchen with the calf, I watch as she digs through the fridge and pulls out a bunch of fruit and vegetables, offering them to the cow one by one, and when she shoves a carrot in its confused little face, I roll my eyes and shake my head. It's not a fucking rabbit. It probably needs milk . . . from it's goddamn mother.

As if having the same thought, she pulls out the carton of milk, and with just one look at it, there's no denying that that's not going to be enough for that little calf. I'll have to stop by Bessy's store and get some more while we figure out how to actually feed this thing properly, because let's face it, I'm going to walk in there and Blair is going to bat those thick lashes at me and I'm not going to be able to stop until we have a fucking zoo living inside our house.

I watch Blair for a minute as she tries to figure out how to actually give the milk to the calf, and as she pours the milk into a bottle before attaching a latex glove to the top and using the finger as the teet, I'm blown the fuck away. That was genius. But also, I'm going to have to add cow milk bottles to my shopping list.

It's messy, but she eventually manages to feed the little guy, and as it annihilates every last drop, I watch as Blair reaches for her phone on the table and starts shooting off a text.

My phone chimes barely a second later.

Blair - Could you pick up milk on the way home?
Blair - Like maybe a lot of milk.

I grin, more than ready to drag this out.

Nick - A lot? Why do you need so much milk? You barely drink it as it is.
Blair - Baking. I wanna get into baking.
Nick - Alright. I'll pick up a few bottles of that low-fat milk the doctor suggested.
Blair - NO!
Blair - Whole milk. It has to be whole milk. I need the good shit.

I laugh to myself, watching Blair throw her phone down as the calf finishes off the bottle, and knowing that won't keep him full for long, I get a move on, not wanting to risk the little guy getting aggravated when he comes looking for more.

After picking up every single bottle of whole milk Bessy has in her store and having to then explain what the hell I wanted it for, I get my ass back home. I haven't been able to check in on the security footage since I've been driving, but as I get home and walk through the front door, I find it suspiciously quiet.

"Blair?" I call out, striding through the house and dumping the million bottles of milk onto the counter. "Where are you?"

"Oh shit," I hear from somewhere deeper in the house. "You're home already?"

"What are you doing?"

"I uhhh . . . nothing," she calls out as I hear a flurry of movement along with a shitload of thumping, and is that . . . sloshing? I barely get a chance to turn around before I hear her racing down the hall. She comes into view, completely drenched. "I was on top of all my work so I thought I'd do a deep clean of the bathroom."

My brow arches. "You managed to get on top of all that work?" I question, having seen the mountain of paperwork piled up on her desk this morning and knowing damn well she couldn't have gotten through that in a single month, let alone a single morning. Though, now that she's finally found the strength to visit her nana at her gravesite, she's been spending a lot of time over there, sometimes spending hours sitting against the headstone while working away on her laptop.

This new business of hers has taken off in a huge way, and she's already had to start searching for a virtual assistant. Not to mention, all the underpaid employees at SC Corporate Management were more than happy to jump ship, and so were a few big-ticket clients. She's barely had this business running for three months and she's already making a great name for herself. She'll be the one to watch out for.

"Uh-huh."

"Oh cool. In that case, I'll come and help you with the bathroom."

Blair balances, discreetly shifting her weight onto her other foot, the move putting her directly in the center of the hallway, blocking my way. "No, there's no need for that. Why don't you go change out of your work clothes and we'll spend the afternoon together? Far away from here. Far, far away."

"No, really. We'll get it done in no time if I help."

Her gaze darts around the house as if madly searching for an excuse, and all I can do is lean back against the kitchen counter, crossing my feet at the ankles, getting way too much enjoyment out of this. "You wouldn't be hiding something from me, would you?" I accuse. "Something like a big fucking cow that happens to be chilling in our bathroom?"

Her eyes widen like saucers, gaping at me for just a moment. "How the hell did you know?"

"The security cameras, babe. I knew what you were planning on doing with that cow before you even did. And for the record, we can't keep him. What the hell would we even do with a cow?"

"Love him, Nick," she says, hitting me with those big beautiful eyes . . . and cue the batting lashes. I'm a goner. She steps into me, looping her arm through mine. "At least come and meet him before you go and make a hasty decision. He's sweet."

I groan and let Blair drag me down to the bathroom, and when she reaches for the door and gives me a promising smile, I prepare for the worst. Only as she swings the door open, my jaw drops.

I was expecting a lot of things—a cow getting a facial, maybe it was getting a blowout, or having its hooves painted, but I wasn't expecting to see the little fucker soaking in my bathtub like a goddamn queen.

"What in the fresh hell?"

"He was filthy," Blair says. "We can't have him living here if he's going to stain all the couches."

"Why the hell would he be anywhere near my couches?"

"You don't expect him to sleep on the floor, do you?" she demands before answering her own question. "No, you're right. The couch is insane. He probably couldn't get up there yet. We should buy him a bed . . . or maybe just the mattress. Do you think he needs toys like a dog?"

I stare at the woman I have every intention of making my wife the second she allows me to. "You want to go and buy a mattress for a cow?"

Blair grins and steps into me, her hand cradling the non-existent bump at her stomach. "If Butterscotch is going to be a part of our family and be our baby's sibling, then why the hell shouldn't we give him an incredible life?"

"Butterscotch?" I question, glancing over at the cow who seems to be watching me a little too closely.

"That's his name," she confirms. "Well, either that or Guzzle Guts. You should see the way this thing drinks his milk. It's insane."

A smile pulls at my lips, and I pull her into me. "You really want to be cow parents?"

Blair pouts out her bottom lip before glancing back at the calf. "Look at that little face," she tells me. "How could you possibly send him back out into the world to fend for himself when we can give him the best life any cow could want? Just think of him as an oversized puppy."

"An oversized puppy comes with oversized shits."

She grins wide, knowing she's got me exactly where she wants me. "But he also comes with an oversized heart," she whispers, pushing up onto her tippy toes and brushing her lips over mine. "Just like yours."

Fuck.

Letting out a heavy sigh, I groan and reach for a towel. "Come on, then," I say, nodding toward Butterscotch. "Dry him up. If we leave in the next twenty minutes, we'll be able to catch the pet store before it closes."

"YES!" Blair cheers, yanking the towel out of my hands and hurrying toward the cow. "We're going to be the best cow parents. You're not going to regret this."

Then as she struggles to get the cow out of the tub, I have no choice but to climb in there with it and scoop its heavy ass out of the water. "I already am," I tell her, and yet, I can't fucking wait to see exactly where this goes.

THE NAUGHTY LIST

Thanks for reading

If you enjoyed reading this book as much as I enjoyed writing it, please consider leaving an Amazon review to let me know.

For more information on The Naughty List, find me on Facebook –

www.facebook.com/sheridansbookishbabes

Stalk me

Join me online with the rest of the stalkers!!
I swear, I don't bite. Not unless you say please!

Facebook Reader Group
www.facebook.com/SheridansBookishBabes

Facebook Page
www.facebook.com/sheridan.anne.author1

Instagram
www.instagram.com/Sheridan.Anne.Author

TikTok
www.tiktok.com/@Sheridan.Anne.Author

Subscribe to my Newsletter
https://landing.mailerlite.com/webforms/landing/a8q0y0

More by Sheridan Anne

www.amazon.com/Sheridan-Anne/e/B079TLXN6K

DARK CONTEMPORARY ROMANCE - M/F
Broken Hill High | Haven Falls | Broken Hill Boys
Aston Creek High | Rejects Paradise | Bradford Bastard
Pretty Monster (Standalone)

DARK CONTEMPORARY ROMANCE - REVERSE HAREM
Boys of Winter | Depraved Sinners | Empire

NEW ADULT SPORTS ROMANCE
Kings of Denver | Denver Royalty | Rebels Advocate

CONTEMPORARY ROMANCE (standalones)
Play With Fire | Until Autumn (Happily Eva Alpha World) | The Naughty List (Christmas Romantic Comedy)

PARANORMAL ROMANCE
Slayer Academy [Pen name - Cassidy Summers]

Printed in Great Britain
by Amazon